Zinforado!

Zinforado!

By
Mike Stepanovich

Copyright © 2017 Michael J. Stepanovich

Publisher: Que Sirah Syrah

www.zinforado.com

Contact the Author: mike@zinforado.com

Cover design by Glenn Hammett
Photos by Greg Iger

Printed in the United States of America

ISBN: 978-0-692-83390-2

Table of Contents

Foreword i
Cast of Characters iii
Chapter 1 1
Chapter 2 13
Chapter 3 15
Chapter 4 37
Chapter 5 41
Chapter 6 51
Chapter 7 69
Chapter 8 77
Chapter 9 103
Chapter 10 111
Chapter 11 125
Chapter 12 139
Chapter 13 175
Chapter 14 179
Chapter 15 181
Chapter 16 183
Chapter 17 189
Epilogue 195
Acknowledgements 197
About the Author 201

Foreword

I have been involved with the wine industry as a wine writer, wine judge and wine educator since 1985. I even made my own wine for 12 vintages in an effort to gain a greater understanding of this delightful beverage.

People are always asking me what's my favorite wine and vintage.

I always tell them wine is my favorite wine.

As for my favorite vintage, I hope I haven't tasted it yet.

But in my lifetime, so far, my favorite vintage is 1991. Mother Nature dealt a remarkable hand that year. The growing season started early, cruised through a moderate summer, and extended well into fall. It was a Rolls Royce of a vintage. I made quite an effort to acquire 1991 wines; the ones I have been opening recently are still ascending. It was a splendid vintage that produced splendid wines.

This is a story about one of those wines...

ZINFORADO!

ii

Cast of Characters:

– **Cornelius Reece Kildeer**, nickname Cork, owner of Kildeer Ranch Winery.

– **Catherine Mary Phairfield Kildeer**, Cork's wife, nickname Cathy.

– **J. Worthington Smythe**, writer/publisher of Wines by Smythe newsletter, reviews.

– **Bobby Vangree**, the Kildeers' friend and small-winery owner.

– **Dudley Samples**, publisher/owner of The Wine Bung, monthly wine magazine.

– **Will Weinglas**, Wine Bung senior editor/writer.

– **Laura Troublante**, ruthless lawyer, owner of Troublante Vineyards.

– **Mindy Surlees**, assistant to Laura Troublante.

– **Millie Bounty**, motherly owner of The Boobsie Twins restaurant.

– **Travis R. "TR" Ellis**, local vintner and friend of the Kildeers.

ZINFORADO!

Chapter 1

FRIDAY, APRIL 1, 1994

Cork wasn't his real name, but everybody called him that.

It beat his real name, which for the life of him he couldn't figure out why his parents had given him. The day of his birth must have been a hell of a celebration, he mused, or a hell of an argument.

Cornelius Reece Kildeer was in a hurry now, his purposeful strides carrying him toward his small winery building where in just a few minutes "God" personified was going to pass judgment on his wines.

So if Cork Kildeer seemed a little preoccupied, it was understandable.

Cork didn't think of himself as a great winemaker. A farmer was more like it. Just good local stock, a high school star athlete at Oak Pass High on California's Central Coast who went on to the University of California at Davis determined to be something other than what his parents had been.

But here he was, back on the family land, trying to make a living as best he could, running the family business since his parents had decided that tending grapevines was tiresome.

Actually he thought, as he reached the winery door and stepped into the humid coolness, it was a pretty good life after all. He didn't have the big mortgage on the property that so many others had. He had existing customers when he started. Really, all he had to do was maintain what had been handed to him.

And he was plenty adept at that. Hell, he'd been pruning the gnarled old zinfandel vines that covered the 80-acre ranch since he was 8 years old or so. These oldsters, planted shortly before Prohibition by some long-forgotten soul who apparently didn't believe that anybody in his right mind would prohibit alcoholic beverages, were like wrinkled old hands stretching out of the ground reaching for the sky.

And those old vines bore wonderful fruit. For years, first his grandfather, who purchased the property just before Prohibition ended on a hunch that wine grapes might be a good commodity, and then his father made a pretty comfortable living farming the ranch and selling the fruit to surrounding vintners.

Kildeer Ranch fruit commanded top prices, too. Both Granddad Kildeer and Dad Kildeer had been superb viticulturists. They figured, and rightly so, that if you grow the best quality grapes you can expect the best prices. And their old vines produced a consistent two tons to the acre, perfect for the quality level they sought.

But as California's wine industry began to grow in the late 1960s and into the '70s, the elder Kildeers, shy men who shunned the spotlight, took steps to ensure that they wouldn't be bothered much by tourists and freeloading wine writers looking for free samples and waxing poetic on what the Kildeers viewed as a simple mealtime beverage and nothing more. *Père* Kildeer arranged contracts with enough vintners that the vintners wouldn't have enough Kildeer Ranch fruit for a separate bottling, or if they did, it would be too small to be commercially viable.

But sons always think they've got a better idea, and Cork was struck with the same thought that strikes most all growers eventually: why watch someone else make wine out of your fruit when you can make it yourself?

So in the early '80s, armed with his degree in fermentation science, a new wife and a renewed love for the land, he began pestering his father about building a winery – just a small one, Dad – until finally his father, who was looking to retire anyway, said OK, son, it's all yours and good luck.

Cork wasn't interested in a big winery; a couple thousand cases a year tops would do fine. And Kildeer Ranch had such a good reputation as a grower of top-quality grapes that when it came to naming his winery, there was only one logical choice: Kildeer Ranch Winery.

The prudently managed family business had sufficient reserves to erect a plain-vanilla, no-frills winery building that would serve his needs. The monuments to self were up north; the Central Coast remained rural country, and excess didn't wear well here.

The building had space to accommodate about 100 barrels, about a third again the winery's current production. The roofline on the west wall extended to cover a crush pad, along with an elevated concrete pad for open-top fermenters. The elevated pad allowed Cork to use a gravity-flow system to fill his barrels once fermentation was complete.

But there was more to Cork's strategy than simply making wine from his own fruit. He thought that with the wine boom in full swing – lots of rich folks were busily turning big fortunes into small ones in their rush to embrace the wine-country lifestyle – it would be a good idea to diversify the business, or at least broaden it.

So one by one, he let the grape contracts lapse, until he had three left that he restructured to give each of the three wineries fruit from 15-acre blocks, leaving 35 acres for himself. This would allow them to make vineyard-designated wines, which Cork thought was a good marketing plan. Having others say they made wine from your fruit was great advertising.

Four years ago, he had made his first wine from Kildeer Ranch fruit – his very own grapes. And they were beautiful grapes, perfectly ripe – remarkable for zinfandel – beautifully balanced, a spectacular wine. He was proud of his first effort, and a little awed, too. How much was beginner's luck? After all, he really hadn't done much winemaking since returning to the ranch from college. He'd helped at some of the neighboring wineries to keep his hand in, to talk with friends and neighbors and to learn, but still it wasn't like doing it full time, and he knew it.

But that first vintage, 1990, had been a doozy, and while he had only sold it locally and shared it with his winemaking pals, he still had a sense that others had been as impressed by it as he was.

His second vintage was even more impressive, a truly magnificent wine that in truth he had only shared up to this point with a few close friends. It excited and scared him at the same time because he knew it was more than just a simple mealtime beverage. It was world-class.

And now "God" was coming to taste it and barrel samples of the next two vintages.

He grabbed a 4-foot length of quarter-inch rubber hose lying on top of an empty barrel that he used for a bench, a couple of empty bottles, and made his way through the maze of stacked oak barrels to the ones he would tap for the tasting.

As the first one was filling, he heard the door open and turned to see Cathy Kildeer coming toward him.

"Hi, cutie," she said with a wink.

Wondrous Cathy. They had met their sophomore year at Davis. He was the country kid from the Central Coast, she the sophisticated debutante from San Francisco who before she enrolled at Davis thought milk came from cartons, and lettuce was something you said just before you prayed. Her parents had wanted their daughter to attend Stanford, but underestimated her resolve to go her own way.

Catherine Mary Phairfield majored in English because honestly, she didn't know what career path to choose. She had a vague idea of teaching, or perhaps marketing, but wanted to keep an open mind and see where life took her. She thoroughly enjoyed the many general education classes – philosophy, economics, biology, chemistry and more. College was a revelation for her. She was one of those rare souls who trusted her heart and was willing to go where it directed her rather than follow artificial goals – college, job, marriage – established by convention.

Cathy had thoroughly smitten young Cork Kildeer, and she was equally taken with him. Almost from the moment they met, Cathy's heart took her straight into Cork's arms. Before long the two of them commenced a mutual study of human anatomy; they thought they had invented sex, and worked to perfect the invention. They made an attractive couple, the athletic, 6-foot-tall Cork and the petite, buxom Cathy.

She had captivated his parents when he first brought her home, and embraced the Kildeers' lifestyle as if it was something she had been seeking all her life.

Her parents weren't so happy with the union. Cork was polite and well spoken, but preferred 501s and boots to Bermuda shorts and Topsiders. And when they learned he was taking their darling daughter to the Central Coast, well, that was just too much. They sought refuge at their country club bar, wondering where they had gone wrong.

Cathy just ignored their objections. Whatever the future had in store for her, it would be with Cork, she knew that. She loved him. The rest would come; she wasn't worried.

Cathy and Cork were best friends, lovers, and soul mates. In short, they were a perfect match.

Staring at her now, in her tight Levi's and sleeveless blouse, Cork couldn't believe how lucky he was. She saw the temptation in his eyes and smiled.

"Sue just called, and he's left their place," she said. "Should be here in a half hour or so. You ready?"

Cork snapped out of his reverie and took a deep breath. "I guess," he said. Then he shook his head. "I can't believe how everybody jumps when this guy says frog. Can you believe the influence of this guy?"

"It *is* hard to comprehend," she said. "Here, I'll take that bottle back to the house; you bring the other one when you're done."

The Kildeers had no tasting room per se. Kildeer Ranch Winery was a low-tech affair. Tasting in the winery was done on a couple of rough-hewn planks atop a couple of upright barrels. For occasions such as this one, Cork and Cathy usually took the samples back to their kitchen a short distance away, which doubled as the winery's lab.

A couple minutes later Cork joined Cathy in the kitchen, and they began setting up glasses in preparation for the arrival of J. Worthington Smythe,

the god of all wine critics, whose monthly newsletter, Wines by Smythe, could – fairly or not – break a winery with sharp enough criticism, or, indeed, make it just as quickly.

Smythe, at that moment, though, was lost. It's hard to lose yourself in a 15,000-population town, especially one where the blocks are square. But Smythe had managed to do just that, much to his annoyance. He didn't like being amidst the great unwashed.

He was born with a silver spoon in his mouth to a well-to-do family in Manhattan and grew up wanting for nothing. A bright lad, he attended the right prep schools and graduated from Yale with a degree in accounting; shortly thereafter he became a certified public accountant. He joined a prestigious accounting firm uptown, and would have been quite happy there, except that he discovered he had another great talent.

His family had routinely served wine at the dinner table while he was growing up, so he, his brother and sister were no strangers to it, especially French wines.

It was while he was in college that he discovered he could pick out a myriad of flavors in wine, something his friends weren't able to do. Soon he was giving advice to friends and was the one ordering the wines at dinner parties – French wines of course.

Wines by Smythe started as a small, one-sheet occasional mailing to better serve his friends, and before long grew to a monthly subscription publication that explored wines in depth, offering recommendations and rankings based on a 100-point scale. French wines of course.

But the increasing popularity of California wines and the increasing requests he received to review

California wines prompted him with some niggling reluctance to examine wines he viewed as not much more than rank imitations of the real thing, the real thing being French wines, of course.

But he, along with the rest of the world, sat up and took note when California wines scored particularly well at the so-called Great Paris Shootout in 1976. Imitations or not, he figured he better pay attention to the upstarts.

And his unerring palate continued to serve him well, elevating Wines by Smythe to legendary status. If he said a wine was an 89 instead of a 90, well, it was an 89. His judgment simply wasn't questioned.

Other publications imitated him, most notably The Wine Bung, a monthly slick magazine that included reviews, columns and features, and quickly gained a following among the wine crowd. It irritated Smythe that The Bung had as much influence as it did, particularly when he overheard comments such as, "The Bung gave this wine an 87," or "The Bung gave this one a 91." Usurpers, he thought.

But no matter how much influence The Bung wielded – and it had gained considerable in the last few years – Smythe was the unquestioned authority. He knew it, and so did everybody else.

He had come to the little town of Oak Pass because he kept hearing of the success the area's wines were having in competitions. Except for zinfandel, it was a relatively new region with lots of different varieties planted – cabernet sauvignon, merlot, cabernet franc, sangiovese, nebbiolo, chardonnay, sauvignon blanc, viognier, syrah, barbera – you name it.

He could well have ignored Oak Pass, except that he knew The Bung would eventually find its way there and pass judgment, making it difficult for him. Best to be first and let the others follow.

But he was lost and had pulled into a hamburger joint to get directions from one of the yokels there. A scrawny high-school girl and a pimply-faced kid had given him directions after arguing back and forth over which freeway exit to take.

What a dreadful experience, he mused, finally on the right road, having to deal with these, these philistines!

And now he was on his way to some new winery – Kiljoy, something like that – that half a dozen winery folks around Oak Pass insisted he shouldn't miss if he wanted to taste good zinfandel.

Well, he'd be a killjoy for these rubes, dash their hopes, and the wine world would be better off for it. Besides, he much preferred plying the carpeted monuments in Napa Valley than the linoleumed places on the Central Coast where the locals weren't as deferential.

He exited, and after crossing under the freeway, turned right onto a parallel frontage road that gradually veered about a quarter mile or so away from the freeway. He saw the small Kildeer Ranch sign telling him the winery's driveway was 500 feet ahead on the left. Slowing, he turned onto the gravel driveway.

Straight ahead of him was Cork and Cathy's house, while on the right was the winery building. A low rock wall surrounded the Kildeers' front yard, with several rose bushes sporting their spring blooms. A carport on the home's south side accommodated the Kildeers' car and pickup. The graveled open area between their home and winery allowed for visitor parking and grape-laden trucks to circle the winery and drop their load at the crush pad before exiting to the driveway. The 80-acre vineyard extended on their property to the east and south of the house and winery.

Cathy spotted the rented Lincoln Towncar as it pulled up in front of their house, and J. Worthington Smythe alighted, wearing his Cardigan sweater and bow tie.

Growing up in San Francisco society helped her now. Smoothly and graciously – despite the Levi's – she went out to greet Smythe.

"Mr. Smythe," she cooed, walking out the front door, hand extended, "I'm so glad to meet you. Won't you come in? Would you like some refreshment before we start, some iced-tea perhaps?"

Her warm smile and wholesome good looks caught Smythe off-guard, and melted some of his contrived ice. "Well, uh, yes, thank you," he stammered.

She introduced him to her husband, whose friendly country ways further melted him and his resolve to give them a good screwing, although he still felt the bumpkins needed a comeuppance.

The iced tea was good – sun-tea, he noted – and helped wash the town's bad taste from his mouth.

But he was totally unprepared for what happened next.

Sitting down at the kitchen table – how absolutely plebian, he thought – Smythe had three wine glasses lined up in front of him.

"We only have a few bottles of our '90 zin left, so we're starting you with our '91," Cathy said, pouring the first glass, followed by the next two with the barrel samples Cork had drawn earlier.

Smythe picked up the first glass, swirled it, and was immediately impressed with its dark purple color. He put it to his nose and inhaled.

My God! he thought, what fantastic aromas. He started ticking them off: cinnamon, allspice, cardamom, boysenberry, black cherry, thyme, cedar, tobacco, black olive, and classic black pepper. He couldn't believe it.

He took a sip, and thought he would go into orgasmic convulsions, the flavors were so incredible – all that he had picked up in the nose and more! The wine filled his mouth with complex flavors and the finish was so long he thought it would reach right down to his toes.

He forgot all about hosing the Kildeers. He was simply flabbergasted, overcome. He had never tasted another wine like it. He took another sip, with the same explosion of flavors. Incredible! he thought. Unreal!

He came out of his reverie to find Cork and Cathy looking at him intently, expectantly. Suddenly he was suspicious: this had to be a ringer. A zinfandel couldn't be *THAT* good.

"Where are the rest of the bottles?" he asked.

"Over in the winery," Cork said.

"Can you pull another one?" Smythe asked.

Cork and Cathy looked at each other, and shrugged. "Sure," Cork said. "Bring your glass and follow me."

They went out the side door, across the gravel driveway and into the winery. In a corner were the 1,200 or so cases of Kildeer Winery's 1991 vintage. At Cork's gestured invitation, Smythe went over, opened a case, took a bottle and put it on the two-plank tasting bar. Cathy pulled the cork and poured into Smythe's glass.

He swirled, sipped – my God! They were the same! Wine this good just didn't come along every day.

"Estate fruit?" Smythe asked. For an answer, the Kildeers led him out the door and Cork pointed to the gnarly vines.

"When were these planted?"

"About 1916," Cork said.

Seventy-eight years old, Smythe thought. "Your family?"

"No, someone else. We don't really know much about him. We don't know what clones these are or where they came from. My grandfather bought the property in 1933 for back taxes. No one seems to know what happened to the guy who originally planted it. But we've taken good care of the vineyard since then."

Smythe nodded. You sure as hell have, he thought.

They returned to the kitchen where Smythe, almost trancelike, tasted the barrel samples from the '92 and '93 vintages. He noted the differences in his notebook and that while not quite reaching the level of the '91, they were easily in the 95-100 range as well.

He finished the '91 sample, thanked the Kildeers for their time, walked out the front door, climbed into his rented tank and drove off.

Cork and Cathy looked at each other, shrugged, and started talking about the great god of wine who to them looked more like a snob than anything else. They laughed, washed the glasses, and finished the bottle of '91, which led to an afternoon of anatomical study.

Chapter 2

TUESDAY, APRIL 5

Back in his New York office, Smythe wrote his review. He was so excited that even the long flight home hadn't tired him. He couldn't wait to get this issue to the printer. Those nitwits over at The Bung would be falling all over themselves trying to catch up.

I have discovered a little-known winery, where nature has conspired to create some special grapes. This micro-winery has lovingly taken those grapes and created a wine so balanced, so delicious, so wonderful, that mere words can't do it justice.

I have only given one other perfect score since begin-ning my publication, to a great, great Burgundy. But only through my ranking can the consumer get an idea of Kildeer Ranch Winery's truly incredible achievement.

• 1991 Kildeer Ranch Winery Estate Zinfandel – Score: 100.

ZINFORADO!

Chapter 3

TUESDAY, APRIL 12

Cork and Cathy were still asleep when the first phone call came.

It hadn't even been two weeks since J. Worthington Smythe had visited them, but they'd pretty much forgotten about him.

"Mr. Kildeer?" the voice asked, as Cork peered at the alarm clock, trying to figure out who would be calling him at 4:30 in the morning.

"Yes, who's this?" Cathy was stirring now.

"William Johnston's my name. I'm calling you from New Haven."

"New Haven?" Cork was still half asleep.

"Connecticut. I just saw the write-up about you. I wanted to order some of your '91 zinfandel before you sold out."

"Well it's 4:30 in the morning here. Why don't you call back around 8:30 or 9."

"Uh, sorry, I forgot about the time difference. But since I'm on the phone, can't you just take my order?"

"No. I'm going back to sleep."

"But I'm calling you from 3,000 miles away!"

"And I'm sleeping 3,000 miles away. G'night Mr. Johnston." And he hung up.

Twenty minutes later, the phone rang again. This time it was some cracker in Florida.

"Are you the fella who got a hunnert for his zin-fan-dell?" the caller asked.

Cork was still groggy but slightly more awake this time. He thought the caller was talking price.

15

"Well, our zin is $15 a bottle, but with a case discount it'll come to a little more than $150 a case."

"Tha's fahn, but are you the raht fella? Is your wine the one that scored a hunnert?"

"A-what? Why are you calling me now? It's, let's see" – he looked at the digital clock – "4:53."

"Ah know what time it is. It's 7:53 where Ah am, and Ah wants to make sure Ah get some of that wine – if you're the raht fella. Are you?"

"Sir, I don't want to be rude, but you're the second person who's called and waked me up, and I'm not sure what you're talking about. So please, call back during business hours."

He heard "But wait ..." as he hung up the phone.

What the heck was going on, he wondered, which is exactly what Cathy asked him no sooner had he thought it.

"I don't know, but that last guy asked if we were the ones who got a hundred for our zinfandel. No, let's see, he said did we score a hundred."

"You don't think it could be that guy Smythe, do you?" Cathy asked.

"A hundred from him? That would be hard to believe. I mean it's a good wine, but nobody ever gets a hundred from him. Nobody ever gets 99, or even 98."

Just then the phone rang again, at 5:05. "Let me answer this one," said Cathy, reaching across her husband. "Hello?"

"Hello, is this Kildeer Ranch Winery?" a woman asked.

"Yes it is, but we won't be open for another four hours. Why are you calling at this hour of the morning?"

"Oh, I'm sorry. It's a little after 8 here. I just ..."

"Where's here?" Cathy asked.

"Manhattan."

"Kansas?" Cathy knew full well the caller wasn't referring to the home of Kansas State University, but she loved to tweak New Yorkers. And anyone calling at 5:05 in the morning was going to get a tweak.

"New York!" the woman said, her tone one of exasperation and astonishment.

"New York? Isn't that a state back east somewhere?" She and Cork were both stifling laughs.

"City! New York City!"

"Well why are you calling at this hour?"

There was a pause; the woman, who was thinking she'd called an imbecile, had almost forgotten why she had called. "Uh, I just read the review of your '91 zinfandel in Wines by Smythe and wanted to order some. How much is available? I'll buy as much as you'll sell me."

"Really? I haven't seen the review yet. What'd it say?"

"You really don't know?"

"No."

"He gave you 100. A perfect score. Do you know that only one other wine has ever gotten 100 from him? And that was a great French Burgundy. Honey, you must have some kind of wine to get 100 from Smythe. Now how much can I get?"

Cathy was stunned. She covered the mouthpiece and whispered to Cork, "She says Smythe gave us 100 for the '91."

"What!?!" Cork sat up in bed. "I can't believe it!"

"Hello? Hello?" Cathy heard the New Yorker on the phone.

"I'm sorry, but this is pretty exciting news for us. Plus we're still in bed. Can you call us back after 9 – noon your time?"

"Uh, well..."

"Thank you so much. Goodbye," Cathy cooed, and hung up.

"A hundred!" Cork was still dazed. "Nobody gets a hundred from him."

"That's pretty amazing," Cathy said, leaning back on the pillow with her hands behind her head. "That woman said he's only given a hundred to one other wine, a French one."

Cork was now fully awake. He was well aware of reviewers' influence on consumers. He knew that a good review or a good showing at a wine competition could boost sales substantially. A hundred from Smythe? That would likely put their sales in the stratosphere.

"Do you realize what this will do for us?" he said. "We're going to get swamped, if these calls are any indication." He glanced at his wife. "Remember that cartoon in a magazine I showed you a few months back? It kind of sums up what's about to happen."

"Which one was it, babe?"

"It was the one where a guy walks into a tasting room, and the snob behind the bar is polishing wine glasses, nose firmly in the air. The snob pours a taste. The guy tries it and gags. 'That's awful, worst stuff I've ever had!' he says. The snobby guy says, 'Smythe gave it a 93.' The guy says, 'I'll take a case.' Anyway, that's what I think is about to happen to us, people buying it just on his say so."

Just then the phone rang again.

And it only got worse.

By 6:30, the central time zone had kicked in, and by 7:30 the calls were coming about as soon as they hung up from the previous one. Finally, in desperation, they left the phone off the hook.

Sitting in the kitchen with a cup of coffee, their plight began to sink in.

"I think we're in trouble," Cork said. "I can't believe all these people wanting our wine."

Cathy knew her husband was worried that a quiet, pristine lifestyle had just been shattered. She was worried about it, too. Because even though she was a city girl and loved visiting cities, she had grown to appreciate the tranquility and solitude their rural life offered. She, maybe more than he, knew their life was about to change – had already changed – dramatically.

"C'mon," she said, picking up her coffee cup, motioning him to do the same. They walked out the back door, and, hand-in-hand, crossed the small backyard and open expanse to the edge of the vineyard and stood there in the morning sun gazing eastward over the old vines that had very suddenly changed their lives.

The vineyard was on a broad alluvial plain adjacent to the Upsidedown River. Over many centuries, the river had flooded countless times, depositing rocks and gravel and silt across the acreage that was now Kildeer Ranch. The land was virtually unfarmable for row crops or grains, and the minimal amount of grass that did manage to sprout on it wouldn't support any kind of livestock.

The forgotten fellow who figured the land was good for grapes had had a tough time planting it. Old-timers said it took twice as long to plant as any other vineyard because it was so tough digging through the alluvial "soil," the source of the rocks for the low wall around the home's front yard.

But crummy soil makes great vineyards, and this was no exception. The vines struggled to grow, their roots searching down through the gravel and rocks for nutrients and moisture. The vines, convinced they were all going to die, produced remarkable fruit from their first crop on. Of course, during Prohibition, who cared? A few of the locals sneaked into the forgotten vineyard and carted off what fruit there was for some homemade wine – you were allowed to make 200 gallons for personal use.

Randall Kildeer, Cork's grandfather, understood the vineyard's potential – and that Prohibition was about to end. So in mid-1933 when the property came up for auction by the county for back taxes, he bid on it – the only bidder, it turned out.

Under three generations of Kildeer care, the old vines had flourished, rewarding their caretakers with a solid if not flashy living.

Cork and Cathy gazed out over the gnarled, weather-beaten old vines, instinctively knowing that their peaceful life was about to end and wanting to cling to the moment for as long as they could.

The moment lasted about two minutes more before they heard a vehicle turning down their driveway.

Walking around the north side of their house, they saw it was none other than Bobby Vangree.

Bobby had a small operation, Clover Leaf Cellars, a few miles east of Oak Pass on the road to the great central valley. He was a funny guy, a bon vivant, ladies man. He was also a good-hearted soul who would give the shirt off his back to help a friend.

Bobby was Cork's best friend. His dad had died when Bobby was young and his mom, Sarah, had to work several jobs in local restaurants and wineries. She was relieved when Cork's family took the rambunctious Bobby on family outings and had him over regularly for dinner.

Bobby's life might have looked hard from the outside, but the boy didn't seem to notice. He had a knack for finding a good time no matter where he was.

And Cork, by nature somewhat circumspect, was happy to be included in the fun.

When he and Cork were about 10, they discovered an old landfill site one summer day and spent weeks picking through the refuse to find parts to build a small dirt bike. It was a Frankenstein contraption, but it took them practically all over the county on back roads.

It was Bobby who discovered that old man Burnett was tossing his magazines and other papers in the trash cans awaiting pickup in the alley behind his house. Among the magazines were old issues of Playboy and Penthouse that he and Cork liberated for later perusal in their "fort," a decrepit old shed on the far back side of Cork's family property.

Bobby charged their friends a quarter each to look through the stash until Cork's dad discovered the loot and hauled it off with a weak attempt at a stern warning.

As they went through high school, Cork gravitated to sports, Bobby to the farm programs and mechanics. The guy could fix anything with wheels, Cork marveled. And Bobby was at every game Cork ever played, cheering the loudest and spiking the girls' drinks.

When Cork went off to college, Bobby stayed behind working at various wineries as a cellar rat, vineyard worker – any job he could – shoveling pomace, pruning vines, learning the trade. He stuck with a small, family-owned winery as assistant winemaker/cellar rat for several years, saving his money and bedding every woman he could.

Cork always wondered why it was that women would just hop into bed with guys like Bobby – kind of scrawny and not particularly good looking – while guys like Cork – solid, hard-working, caring – didn't seem to have that kind of luck with women. A certain safety in superficiality, he supposed. One of life's mysteries.

He remembered the time he dropped by T.R. Ellis Winery, one of the places where Bobby worked, to talk about trellising. It was a warm spring day, and Cork and Travis, the owner, were out walking in the vineyard, looking at the trellises Travis had recently installed, when they heard moaning coming from the direction of Travis's irrigation pond.

Walking over the berm they discovered Bobby lying on his back, and a naked young woman astride him, moving up and down for all she was worth, moaning with each thrust.

"Bobby!" said Travis, peering down at the spectacle. "My God! That's, that's Michele Michaelson! That's Billy Michaelson's wife!"

Bobby grinned sheepishly at the two men looking down at him. "Aw hell, TR, he'd understand."

Michele, who appeared to be in ecstasy, didn't miss a beat.

Travis and Cork just shook their heads and walked away.

Now Bobby had started his own winery with his savings, and his new tasting room was reputed to be party central among the Oak Pass wineries.

And Bobby's wines were good. He had been doing more than just laying the local ladies. He had learned his craft.

His lifelong friendship with Cork automatically extended to Cathy when she came into the picture. Bobby never made even the slightest play for Cathy, although that day at Ellis's had shown first hand that all women were fair game for Bobby, married or not. Lothario that he was, Bobby did have his own code of honor in that regard: if the woman was dedicated to her man, it was strictly hands off, literally.

Of course, if a woman was tired of her husband's routine and looking for some spice in her life, Bobby was always happy to help. A regular philanthropist.

Now, as Cork and Cathy stood holding hands, Bobby braked his well-used Toyota pickup to a halt and hopped out. The early morning sun had already banished the springtime chill.

"Hey, Bobby," Cork called out. "How ya doin'?"

"Hey, Cork. Hey, Cathy. I'm doin' great. But, man, I can't believe it about you guys. I just saw Wines by Smythe. I've been trying to call you guys but your line's been busy."

"Yeah, it started ringing about 4:30 this morning," Cathy said. "We finally took it off the hook. It was driving us nuts."

"I can't believe it, you guys! A hundred from Smythe! Can you believe that shit?"

"It's starting to sink in," Cork said.

"You know what you ought to do," Bobby said. "You ought to bump the price up to 50 bucks a bottle for that stuff. It'll still fly outta here. Might as well make hay while you can."

Cathy turned and looked at her husband for a couple of seconds. "He's got something there, babe," she said. "Maybe we should think of doing that."

That was a hard one for Cork. He did not think of himself as a gouger. He charged an honest price for an honest wine, a price that made him a fair profit, and gave the customer a good value. To abandon that philosophy and take advantage of the situation seemed, well, dishonest to him. Yet at the same time, remembering the phone calls this morning from people who couldn't care less what he charged, just so long as he'd sell it to them, the suggestion didn't seem so bad.

"Well, I don't know..." he started to say, rubbing his chin.

"Cork, be smart about this," Bobby said. "You know as well as I do that an awful lot of those wineries up north jack up their price just because of where they are. They don't have any better wine than you or I, but because they're up north they do it, and they get their price, too.

"Now you've got something that most of us can only dream about – something that puts you at an entirely different level, a different price point. For us little guys, reviews and wine competitions help make our reputations. You know that. Go for it!"

Cathy looked at Cork and knew the dilemma he was wrestling with. What would his father say? He hadn't been particularly happy that Cork was making wines, although he had said it's your business now son, you do what you want. He was from the old school. What would he think?

"You know, babe, you've got to do what's right for you," she said softly. "But I think Bobby's right. People are going to be driving in here any time now wanting some of that wine and aren't going to care a whit what they pay for it. All they're going to care is that they got a wine that scored 100. Plus, if we don't we'll be out of wine before the week's out."

"You're probably right," he sighed. "But I don't feel right charging 50 bucks to our friends. Let's charge $50, but for friends, I'll make it half that, $25 a bottle."

"Awrightttt!!!" said Bobby, pumping his fist. "I'll take two cases at that price. Which reminds me, you ought to put away four or five cases right now for your library, otherwise it'll be gone. By the way, how many cases do you have?"

"About 1,200," Cork said.

"Let's see, $50 a bottle, that's $600 a case, and that's ... that's..." he looked thoughtful a moment, "... man, that's almost three-quarters of a million bucks! You just hit the jackpot!"

Dudley Samples was furious. The owner of The Wine Bung was pacing back and forth in his 42nd-story office still digesting the fact that that punk J. Worthington Smythe had just given a wine 100. And not just any wine, a fucking zinfandel of all things! That twit! That dweeb! That abominable asshole!

Now The Bung would have to review the wine, and everybody would be waiting to see what they gave it. Smythe's reputation was such that if The Bung gave it anything less than a 95 the magazine would have immediate credibility problems.

And the worst part about it was that small-fry wineries like Kildeer Ranch didn't advertise. So holding that carrot in front of him – advertise and get a good review – was out. Besides, now Kildeer didn't need to advertise. Goddamn Smythe anyway!

Just then The Bung's senior editor, Will Weinglas, walked into the office. Among other things, Weinglas was in charge of the magazine's wine reviews.

The two were a study in contrasts.

Samples was short, round and a bundle of energy. He dressed well – nothing but suits would do, and starched white shirts – and his neatly trimmed coal-black hair had not a hint of gray. Not even his wife knew that his hair color was due to Grecian Formula.

Truth be told, Samples knew little about wine. Growing up in South Dakota he wasn't exposed to it. His genius was marketing. In high school, his entrepreneurial talent had surfaced. He signed up for a business-class project where students form their own company, sell stock in it, sell their product, and pay the dividends to the shareholders – usually the parents. Samples was so adroit that his company, which sold T-shirts, had more than twice the sales of the second-place team.

He figured out that T-shirts with logos or clever sayings was a growing fad, and after enrolling in college in Chicago, parlayed that fad into a growing fortune. He had the ability to envision all the pitfalls and headaches a small-business owner faces, much like a chess player anticipates moves in advance (he never played chess, either). He left school after a couple years – he never showed up for most of his classes anyway – to conquer more business worlds.

One of those was wine. He recognized in the '70s the American public's growing fascination with wine. Like a bear waking from the long sleep of Prohibition, Americans more and more were looking for sources of information about wine. Samples saw what Smythe was doing, and decided he could do that on a bigger scale. So he founded The Bung. His headquarters was in Chicago, a city he had grown to love for its Midwestern muscle. Besides, he didn't much care for New York. Plus travel was cheaper and less grueling to the West Coast from Chicago.

For Samples, The Wine Bung was business, a niche where he could make some money – lots of it. He understood reviews were what made wineries; the Smythe phenomenon was not lost on him. He also understood that Napa was the American Mecca for wine geeks, and that, fairly or not, all the other wine regions were measured against Napa.

He needed someone who was plugged into the California wine scene, and specifically Napa, and that's where Weinglas came in.

Unlike Samples, Weinglas was tall, 6-foot-2, with a slender build. While he liked sports, he unfortunately was extremely nearsighted, and the thick glasses that constantly slipped down his nose limited his athletic participation. He had tried contacts while in high school but did not like them at all. His nearsightedness made him somewhat self-conscious, and as a result he tended to be initially shy around women, though he enjoyed their company once he felt comfortable with them. His dark brown moppish hair partly covered his ears.

That tendency toward shyness occasionally made him a target of bullies in high school. But they often wished later that they'd left him alone. Weinglas was quiet, observant and patient, a lethal combination for his tormenters.

Trent Harcourt, the high school's much-celebrated quarterback, liked to taunt Weinglas, the team statistician. He went so far as pantsing Wcinglas onc time in the locker room in front of the team.

He laughed and sneered at Weinglas, who was, of course, humiliated, but also annoyed.

Harcourt had a public reputation as a clean-cut Christian boy who loved his mama and his virginal girlfriend, head cheerleader Cindy Blande.

Weinglas knew the football coach wouldn't believe nor care that Harcourt had pantsed the team nerd. But Weinglas, who also helped in the equipment room, knew what went on in the locker room after hours.

He said nothing and waited.

At the next pep rally, when the principal flipped on a video of what he thought was game highlights to charge up the student body, there was Trent naked and panting in the locker room with school slut Hailey Marsh riding him for all she was worth.

"Say my name, bitch! Say it!" Hailey shouted at Trent in the remarkably sharp video.

"H-H-H-Hailey! Hailey! Hailey!" he squealed back.

The auditorium at first fell dead silent as the video looped over and over, but suddenly erupted in wild cheering and laughter. The principal fumbled with the video machine in a vain effort to turn it off, while Cindy Blande, dressed in her cheerleader outfit for the rally, rushed red-faced for the exit, crying. Hailey Marsh beamed, while Harcourt, sitting with the team, seemed to shrink before everyone's eyes.

Weinglas, who was on the school newspaper, had just signed up for the new broadcasting class and was quite proud of his first hidden video footage. He smiled in the raucous auditorium and pushed up his glasses with brisk authority.

Weinglas grew up in a tony section of the East Bay, and early on had learned about wine. It was hard not to, growing up in an area where more wine is consumed per capita than anywhere else in the United States.

He studied journalism at San Jose State, and after graduating he landed a job at a Bay Area newspaper, where a couple years later he began writing a column about wine – Napa, of course, with a smattering of Sonoma thrown in.

Growing weary of the mundane stories his regular reporting job forced upon him, Weinglas answered an ad for a position at The Wine Bung. Samples and Weinglas hit it off almost from the moment they met, and a couple weeks later Weinglas was on The Bung staff.

The two men's sartorial preferences were polar opposites: Samples liked to dress well, and enjoyed social functions, whereas Weinglas adopted the more casual style of his native West Coast – jeans, loafers and open-necked long sleeved shirts with the cuffs rolled up.

But they shared one thing: they both disliked Smythe intensely.

"Dud, can you believe Smythe?" Weinglas said as he burst into the room, pushing up his glasses.

"That shit," Samples snapped. "Now everybody and his brother will be on us about why we haven't done anything on the Central Coast. So once again, Smythe is stirring us. And that pisses me off!"

"Me too," Weinglas echoed. But where Samples had a knee-jerk reaction, Weinglas' journalism training caused him to react more rationally. "We have to do something. Let's scrap next month's cover story and get going on the Central Coast. We've still got time if we get right on it. I can fly out this afternoon, be there tomorrow. I'll line up a photographer to meet me there. We can..."

Samples cut him off. "You don't understand. Laura Troublante is the cover story, and she's paid a bundle in advertising. If we pull her, we're talking big trouble. We simply can't afford it."

"I could talk to her," Weinglas suggested.

"Yeah, you'd like that," Samples grinned. Weinglas pushed up his glasses and grinned back. Laura Troublante was one of the most powerful vintners in the United States – and the most beautiful.

"Well, what do we do, boss?" Weinglas asked. "Gotta do something. You could hold the Troublante package until next issue."

"How good are Troublante's wines?" Samples asked.

"Well, the upper tier aren't bad," Weinglas said, thinking he saw where Samples was going. "We could put her in the low 90s – like 90 or 91 – and nobody would question us, but the regular stuff, the stuff she churns out, isn't all that great – just OK entry-point wines. The trouble is that her 90s-rated stuff is also expensive, whereas this, what is it? this Kildeer zin, is only 15 bucks. It's the type of wine that ordinarily would get reviewed by our second team, the back-room workers. It's a wine I likely wouldn't have tasted."

"That's my point. I think we can do a story about the Central Coast, put it in the back of the magazine – those small-timers won't advertise – review the Kildeer wine, and do what we can to discredit Smythe. I just can't believe the wine's that good.

"Another thing: Laura's having a big reception at the end of this week for the new release of the Troublante reserve meritage. You could go down to Oak Pass, get the story, then meet me up in Napa on Friday for the reception. All the leading lights in Napa will be there and it will be good for us to show up as well. You were going out there for a wine competition next week anyway, weren't you?"

"Yeah, I am," Weinglas smiled, pushing up his glasses. "Not a bad plan, Dud. It'll be a pleasure to put those hayseeds in their place, and maybe shit on Smythe at the same time."

At that moment, Laura Troublante was admiring herself in front of a full-length mirror in her bedroom. She opened her ankle-length satin robe revealing her exquisite body. The owner of Troublante Vineyards was spectacular, if she did say so herself – 5-feet-10, 128 pounds, beautifully tapered thighs, a slim waist and splendid breasts. At 38 years old, she could still pass easily for 28. She worked out regularly, enjoyed a healthy diet, and drove men wild. She lifted each breast, and turned slightly back and forth examining each one. No stretch marks, or signs of sag. Her long, black hair curled at the end just below her shoulders. She smiled as she closed her robe. I could have been a centerfold, she thought.

Laura Troublante had learned early on that she had a body that made men drool – and that properly used she could get just about anything she wanted. She had been a skinny, figureless waif until about eighth grade when Poof! she filled out almost overnight. Unlike many girls who tended to slouch to hide their breasts when they appeared, Laura stood with her back straight, accentuating their lift and curvature all the more. Horny boys were clamoring for dates – she knew what they wanted.

Laura was 14 when she first had sex, and almost instantly learned how to use it as a weapon. She discovered that she liked sex, developed an insatiable appetite for it even. But her realization of how it could be used to manipulate men was even more titillating to her and through the years she perfected that skill.

She was also very bright – valedictorian of her high school class, and sex had nothing to do with it. She made it through Cal in three years, and Stanford law school in two. By the time she was 27 she was already a partner in a prestigious San Francisco law firm. Her meteoric ascent was helped by the fact that in addition to being the hardest working lawyer in the firm, she provided the senior male partners the best sex they ever had.

She was a ruthless litigator. Winning was everything. If her evidence, arguments and strategy didn't work, she wouldn't stop there. One time she initiated sex with a judge in his chambers to get a favorable ruling. The medical malpractice suit should have been a slam dunk for the plaintiff: a doctor who was drunk when he botched what should have been a simple tonsillectomy wound up killing a single mother of two. The judge was a widower who had thrown himself into his work after his wife died in an effort to cope with his grief. Aware of his vulnerability, Laura came into his office, slowly and tantalizingly undressed, and proceeded to seduce him.

The poor man, who hadn't indulged in sex for four years, had no chance. Laura let him think he was a regular stud, even though the judge was about a 20-second man.

Back in court the next day, the judge suddenly changed his mind about certain evidence he would allow from the plaintiff, and before anyone knew it, the case against the doctor folded. The doctor rewarded Laura handsomely.

By the time she was 34, she had more money than she knew what to do with. Her drive compelled her to be the best, to have the best, and to have everyone else know it.

Sure, she was a top lawyer in San Francisco. But that made her one among dozens. She could establish her own firm and take it global. But that kind of gray corporate lifestyle didn't scratch the other side of her personality – the side that delighted in the sensual.

In the early 1990s, the "wine-country lifestyle" and its trappings was making the covers of magazines. Socialites were holding elaborate weddings at estates in Napa. The best hotels and restaurants were emerging up north.

Power, money, notoriety all packaged in a beautiful setting.

She recognized the "wine-country lifestyle" had a certain *je ne sais quoi*, that vintners could attain a sort of star status.

As far as Laura could tell, a beautiful winery in the right location with obscenely priced wine (and the right marketing) were the keys to success.

All she had to do was buy her way in.

And buy she did.

She bought prime Napa Valley property – price was no object – and built an incredible winery: the best equipment, the latest technology, the most beautiful buildings with professional kitchens and enormous dining and reception areas. Everything was first rate.

But she understood that the best equipment in the world is useless if you have poor grapes, so she set about acquiring the best vineyards she could. If money alone wouldn't do it, she added sex – it was almost child's play, men were so easy.

And nobody that she set her sights on held out long, except one wizened old grower who had proved her equal, stretching out the negotiations four months before the combination of a lot of dough and nearly daily sex caused him to capitulate. He was simply exhausted, although his smile at the closing said he was quite satisfied as well. She gave the old guy a mental tip of the hat: he'd been a better lover than most and worked her as hard as she worked him.

But now there was a new challenge: Kildeer Ranch Winery. Obviously, it was a special vineyard. No other American vineyard had ever yielded a 100-point wine. She moved away from the mirror, sat down at the desk in her bedroom, and reread J. Worthington Smythe's review. She noted that the '92 and '93 barrel samples were also highly rated – My God! A 97 and a 98 were astronomical by any standard – which meant that Smythe had truly stumbled onto something.

Her own wines had only ever scored in the high 80s and low 90s. That had put her on the wine world map, but it wasn't the star status she coveted.

And she knew that if Smythe gave a wine a high score it was worth it, because the man simply could not be influenced. She had tried, and concluded the man was asexual. Few men could resist what a view of her ample cleavage and silky thighs promised, but Smythe was one of them.

If she were to be the best, she had to have that vineyard. The question was simply a matter of cost.

She pushed the intercom button on her phone: "Damien, come in here please."

"Right away," was the response.

A few seconds later, a young man bare to the waist and looking like a dancer at Chippendale's appeared. She flicked her hand, and he stepped out of his pants. Then he lay back on the bed. He was already erect by the time she slipped off her robe. She climbed on him and began rhythmically moving up and down.

"I want you to find out everything you can about Kildeer Ranch Winery," she told him. Damien lifted a notepad and jotted down the name. He looked up at her. She was moving much faster now, beginning to get that glazed look of pending orgasmic bliss. Breathing heavily, she continued on: "Call the owners, invite them to the reception this weekend. Learn everything you can about them. Can you have that for me this afternoon?"

"Shouldn't be a problem, Miss Troublante," Damien intoned.

ZINFORADO!

Chapter 4

WEDNESDAY, APRIL 13

"Can you believe it?" Cathy said, as she hung up the phone. "That was Will Weinglas of The Bung. He wants to come interview us, taste the wine."

"Uh-oh," said Bobby Vangree, who had been helping Cork move cases up to the front for easy access. Even at $50 a bottle, the wine had been flying out the door, plus restaurants wanted some for their wine lists. The last couple days had been incredibly hectic. "You know the only reason he's coming is because of Smythe. Hell, those clowns at The Bung don't pay much attention to anything other than Napa and Sonoma unless they have to. And now they have to."

"You're right, Bobby," Cork said. "But what the heck?"

"I told him to drop by tomorrow, babe," Cathy said.

"No problem," Cork replied, hefting another case of wine.

"We also got a call from Laura Troublante. She wants us to come to some reception she's having this weekend."

"Double uh-oh!" Bobby said. "You know what she wants? Your vineyard."

"Why do you say that?" Cork wondered.

"Hell, Cork, that's the way she operates, everybody knows that. What she wants, she buys. And price is no object."

Cork looked at Cathy. Dammit! he thought. But the hand was dealt and they had to play it. People dreamed of getting 100 for their wine, but once you got it, it seemed like it was more trouble than it was worth.

Cathy read the growing frustration in her husband – it was growing in her as well. And she was also becoming alarmed. Bobby's comment had triggered it, and she knew he was right. When Laura Troublante set her sights on something, she usually got it, one way or another – and Kildeer Ranch Winery had apparently come into her crosshairs.

Cork read his wife's thoughts. "Kildeer Ranch Winery is not for sale," he said quietly, looking from Cathy to Bobby, and back to Cathy. "Not for any price."

Bobby looked at Cork and knew he was also thinking about his family, all the effort his father and grandfather and uncles had put into the property. There was tradition here, and how did you put a price tag on that? No matter how much money Laura Troublante offered, it could never add up to the Kildeer family legacy.

But because he knew it didn't mean Troublante knew it, nor would she care.

"You know what you guys need is an ace in the hole," Bobby mused. "You need something to go your way."

"That's funny, Bobby, because most anyone would say getting a hundred from Smythe is having things go your way," Cork said.

"You know what I mean, Cork. You got The Bung showing up here, and you know all they care about is who advertises with them; and you got Troublante ready to pounce. It all adds up to the sharks are circling."

"Yeah, I know. The Bung – I figure that'll play out however it does. It's Troublante I'm worried about."

"I've got an idea," Cathy said suddenly. "Bobby, what are you doing this weekend?"

"Nothing in particular," he replied. "Just hanging out at my tasting room."

"Could you go to Troublante's gig, sort of as our representative?" she asked.

"Sure, I guess so. You want me to see what she has in mind?"

"Yeah, something like that. I'm not really sure, but I'd like to know what's up her sleeve. As far as I know, she never knew we existed before a couple of days ago, and now she's inviting us to this big party."

A smile spread over Bobby's face. He knew Laura Troublante's reputation. It might be fun to give a rich lawyer a screwing for a change.

"Sharon ought to be able to handle the tasting room for a couple of days," he said.

"But now we've got to worry about Weinglas," Cork mused. "You remember when he was out here about three years ago? He really screwed over Travis Ellis. Had him going broke and the last guy down here making cabernet." He shook his head in disgust.

"Oh, I remember him," Bobby said, grinning. "And I've got an idea about how to welcome Mr. Weinglas back to Oak Pass."

ZINFORADO!

Chapter 5

THURSDAY, APRIL 14

Will Weinglas was impressed. Walking into the terminal at Bakersfield's airport he'd spotted the limousine driver holding up the hand-lettered sign with his name on it.

He'd gotten a call the previous day from Bobby Vangree identifying himself as a friend and colleague of the Kildeers. They were looking forward to his visit.

Weinglas had heard vaguely of Vangree; owner of Clover Leaf Cellars, he recalled.

How was he flying in? Vangree had asked. Why not catch the United connection from Chicago to Bakersfield via Denver, he had suggested. Oak Pass was only a little more than an hour's drive from Bakersfield, whereas it was four hours from either Los Angeles or San Francisco. In fact, Vangree had told him, he would have a limo waiting to pick him up in Bakersfield.

The offer appealed to Weinglas' ego. Deal, and thanks, Weinglas had told him.

Weinglas hadn't been to Oak Pass since 1991 when he'd written an article about syrah being the new grape of choice for the area.

He thought about that story during the flight out. In truth, he admitted to himself, the wines in Oak Pass weren't bad at all. In fact some of the vintners were figuring out the right things to plant in the area. Some, like that Ellis character, were still holding out for cabernet sauvignon. But he'd come around. All it took was asking him the same questions three different ways to eventually get the quotes he wanted to fit the story, and the story in these parts was syrah. Weinglas and Samples had established that fact.

He remembered the furious phone call from Ellis insisting he'd been quoted out of context, and that in retrospect the story had been pre-written and all they wanted from him was some quotes. He remembered how Samples had smoothly told him The Bung stood by its story. So what if Ellis had figured it out? Why didn't he just grow some cabbage? Napa was the place for cabernet, and the sooner these rubes realized that the better.

Weinglas really believed that syrah was the best grape for the area, although he'd never grown so much as a radish. He knew zinfandel had historically done well there, and conceded it had a home in Oak Pass, but 100 points? Well, he'd find out soon enough.

Weinglas signaled the limo driver, who appeared not to notice that Weinglas looked a bit rumpled after his flight – Levis, black socks, black penny-loafers, an open-neck long-sleeved light blue shirt – cuffs rolled up, of course – and a navy sport coat that he carried over one arm. His glasses continually slipped down his nose, requiring regular push-ups.

"Right, this way, Mr. Weinglas," the driver said with a smile. "Can I help you with your bag?"

Weinglas handed him his overnighter as they walked through the automatic doors to the curb where a gleaming white Cadillac limousine awaited. The driver put the bag in the trunk and opened the door, motioning for Weinglas to get in.

As he stooped to climb into the car, he saw someone else was inside.

"Hi, Mr. Weinglas, I'm Brandi, the assistant winemaker at Clover Leaf Cellars," said the young woman sitting on the side seat.

"Hello," Weinglas replied rather stiffly. "Nice to meet you."

Weinglas initially felt awkward around women, especially attractive ones, and this one definitely fit that category. Her long blonde hair was pulled back in a ponytail. She was wearing a plaid shirt and jeans. A light sweater was around her shoulders with the sleeves tied around her neck. Her smile was bright and cheery. Smiles like that made him feel self-conscious, and the fact that she had a good figure added to his awkwardness. Consequently, he didn't notice that her hands were soft, her fingernails were long and painted, and her shoes were high heels. Not what one would expect an assistant winemaker to wear.

The driver, a pal of Bobby Vangree's named Art Williams, climbed in and looked in the rearview mirror at The Bung editor's obvious discomfort. He chuckled to himself: dressed just right for what's in store for him. Williams had received a call from Bobby the previous day, asking him to pick up this Weinglas guy.

Bobby had also told Williams to pick up Brandi Monroe for the trip over to Oak Pass. By day Brandi was a college student at Cal State Bakersfield studying business administration. By night she was a dancer in a Bakersfield strip joint where on a good night she cleared 500 bucks.

The idea was to raise Wineglas's blood pressure a notch or two, put him off balance, and pay him back a little for his last visit.

Williams pulled away from the curb, turned out of the airport, drove down to the freeway, and turned west toward Oak Pass.

In the back seat, Brandi was chattering away. She, too, had received a call, giving her a cram course in Wine 101, everything – hopefully – she would need to appear to be an assistant winemaker. Had Mr. Weinglas had a pleasant trip? He must enjoy his work, blah blah blah...

Weinglas was starting to feel a little more comfortable. Monroe was a pleasant sort, although awfully gabby, and it gave him a chance to relax from his flight.

About 15 minutes from the airport, Williams quietly turned on the heater to the passenger compartment. The bright spring sunshine added to the sense of warmth.

A couple minutes later, as the heat started to increase, Brandi, recognizing her cue, said, "Gosh, it's getting a little warm," and undid her sweater, tossing it on the far seat.

Weinglas, too, noticed it was getting warmer, but didn't want to appear uncomfortable, so he just smiled slightly and said nothing.

After a few more minutes – the limo was coming to the foothills separating the great Central Valley and the Oak Pass region – Brandi, who was now carrying on about how she had come to land a job at Clover Leaf Cellars, said, "You know, I really am getting a little warm. I hope you don't mind if I get a little more comfortable." And before Weinglas knew what was happening, she was unbuttoning her shirt and taking it off.

Weinglas was stunned. Before him was this wholesome-looking young woman, who had been telling him about her new job who was suddenly sitting there wearing a black bra that she filled out amply. His jaw dropped.

Brandi seemed not to notice, leaned back, put her arm along the back of the seat, took a deep breath, and said, "Let's see, where was I? Oh, yeah..." and started right in again about the winery.

Weinglas was starting to sweat. What the hell was happening here? Vangree's assistant winemaker certainly wasn't bashful. He was aware of the dampness beginning to spread under his arms, and he could feel a trickle run down behind his left ear, as he pushed his glasses up for the umpteenth time. And his forehead was getting damp. Brandi's voice seemed strangely far away.

A couple minutes later, she said, "You know, it really is warm in here. These jeans are awfully hot." She undid the button and unzipped them, saying, "You gotta wear 'em at the winery, but they're just too heavy here." Brandi kicked off her shoes, and slipped the jeans right off.

Weinglas didn't know what to do. Here was a woman sitting in her bra and matching bikini panties yacking away as if everything was normal. He suddenly didn't know whether it was hot or cold in the car, he just knew he was clammy.

He looked toward the driver to see what he was doing, but he had his eyes on the road – everything normal. What the hell was going on here?

Brandi was telling him how she had gone to Oak Pass after graduation because she thought that would be where the jobs were, and Voila! had found one. Weinglas averted his gaze, looking out the window, feeling very tense.

"I'm not boring you, am I?" she sounded concerned.

He quickly looked back, looking her in the eyes. "Oh no, not at all," he said. He thought about trying to make conversation. "What's your favorite wine?"

"White zinfandel," she said.

"What?! White zinfandel?"

Brandi recognized her misstep: an assistant winemaker wouldn't have white zin as her favorite. Recovering quickly, she said, "That's the wine that first got me interested in winemaking. I still have a soft spot for it. But where we are, cabernet's the thing. I just love our cabernet. It's so, so titillating."

"I'll bet," he thought, suddenly aware of Brandi saying, "Gosh, it's warm, and this bra is awfully confining..."

And just as he was saying "Oh, no!" and putting his hand up in a vain effort to stop her, she reached up, undid the front clasp and slipped the bra off. She then stretched, thrusting her breasts forward as she stretched her arms back.

"Ah, that's better," she said, shaking her breasts gently back and forth before settling back in her seat. "Now, where was I?"

The limousine pulled up in front of the Kildeers' place, and no one was happier to get out of the car than Will Weinglas.

In fact, he hadn't even waited for Williams to come around and open the door. Brandi Monroe had been virtually nude the last 20 minutes of the trip from the airport, which had left Weinglas squirming.

He stood there and realized he was entirely damp. Williams approached him and said, "I'm sorry about the heater, Mr. Weinglas. I'll go back to town to get it fixed and be back for you as soon as I can."

Brandi called from inside the limo, "Bye, Mr. Weinglas, nice talking with you."

Weinglas just nodded glumly, and started walking toward the winery building, where a line of about 20 people stretched from the doorway toward the jammed parking area. Other cars were parked down the driveway leading to the main road. Even then another car pulled off and parked at the end of the line.

The line of customers was there for one thing: to get some of the magic wine. As he approached the doorway, he noticed two large planks had been placed on two upright barrels at the door. A young man was behind the planks taking orders.

Weinglas pushed up his glasses, and walked to the front of the line. "I'm here to see Cork Kildeer," he said. "Do you know where I can find him?"

"Try the house," the kid said.

As Weinglas turned, again reseating his glasses, he spotted a young couple walking his way. As they got nearer, the man said, "Are you Will Weinglas?"

"Yes, that's me," he replied.

"Hi, Cork Kildeer," he said, extending his hand, "and this is my wife, Cathy."

Cathy also shook hands with Weinglas. "We've been expecting you," she said, smiling.

"Well, I guess you want to taste the zinfandel." Cork said.

The zinfandel? Weinglas thought. These arrogant shits. Give 'em a hundred and how do they act? Like they're from Napa. But he said, "Sure."

"OK, c'mon," said Cork as he and Cathy led the way back toward the house. Cork wasn't sure what to expect from Weinglas. The guy had serious B.O., and he wasn't sure what role Bobby Vangree had played in that. Plus, he knew The Bung guys hated Smythe – the whole industry knew that – and suspected that Weinglas was going to try and discredit Smythe, at

47

Kildeer Ranch's expense. Consequently, he didn't feel like doing anything special for the guy. Besides, he thought most wine writers were a bunch of prima donnas who were more impressed with themselves than anything else. From what he'd heard, Weinglas was one of the worst in that regard.

But he felt the wine spoke for itself.

They entered the kitchen. Cork picked up a bottle of the '91 zin from the counter, pulled off the foil and inserted an Ah-so. With a quick twist, he deftly pulled the cork.

Five glasses were on the counter; he took three of them and rinsed them under the faucet, shook off the excess water, put them on the counter and poured the wine.

Don't go all out, Weinglas thought as he picked up his glass. The wine's aroma stopped him dead in his tracks. He had never smelled a wine so complex, so delicious, so ... so ... It was indescribable!

Weinglas didn't know what to think. He'd arrived here in a limo with a naked woman, and now he was smelling wine the likes of which he had never smelled before. He had not been prepared for this.

He took a sip and nearly swooned from the sensation. What a magnificent wine! Absolutely stunning! How to tell Samples? He wouldn't want to hear this.

Suddenly he was aware of Cork and Cathy staring at him, both with slight smiles. He looked back and forth from one to the other – and knew that they knew. Like Smythe, he had been seduced. He swallowed.

"I take it that you like the wine," Cathy said in a soft, almost seductive voice. It wasn't a question.

All Weinglas could do was nod dumbly. Suddenly it struck him: He'd claim that Kildeer was The Bung's find. Smythe had just beaten them to the punch. Jesus! A zinfandel, no less! He swirled and sniffed again; the nose was so heavenly!

No use faking it. He was busted. "Unbelievable!" he mumbled.

Cork and Cathy glanced at each other, then back at Weinglas and smiled, ever so slightly.

"Say, uh, Will, you said you were here to do a story?" Cork asked.

"Uh, yes," Weinglas said, snapping himself out of his reverie. It occurred to him that what The Bung had that Smythe didn't was a story, photos, a literary picture of a couple and their winery. But he'd have to work fast – not much of a problem for him as a former daily journalist – but he'd have to get a photographer here quick, in the next day or so.

Putting on his best smiley face, he pulled out his tape recorder, and after asking the Kildeers if they minded if he taped their interview – they assured him they didn't – he began asking about the ranch, the wine, all the things that would go into the article. The Kildeers told their story while walking around the property, showing him the old vines, the rocky soil sloping down to the river, the winery.

As usually happens, the Kildeers loosened up a bit, and Weinglas warmed up a bit, and after an hour or so, they were all having a pleasant conversation. By now it was getting late in the afternoon, but Weinglas noticed that the line at the tasting room had not abated, if anything, it was longer.

As they walked back toward the house, Cork said, "When do you think this article will come out?"

"Oh, I'm not sure," Weinglas was suddenly cagey again – had to save face. He didn't want to say as fast as I can write it.

Just then the gleaming white limo turned into the driveway, which caused heads to turn in the line. As it pulled into the area between the house and the winery, the sunroof suddenly opened, and Brandi popped out topless, and waving at Weinglas and the Kildeers.

Weinglas pushed up his glasses and turned red. Gawkers in line started whistling and hooting. Brandi beamed as she turned and waved at them.

"Hi, Mr. Weinglas, I'm back," she yelled, seemingly at the top of her lungs. "Are you ready to go? I can't wait to show you around our winery. I know you want to stay abreast of all our developments."

This caused more hooting from the peanut gallery.

Cork and Cathy stared, then looked at each other, stifling a laugh. Weinglas wouldn't have heard anyway. He was crimson from embarrassment, and had started to sweat again. Pretending to be nonplussed, he turned to Cork and Cathy and said as he shook hands, "Well, my ride's here. Thanks for all your help. Be seeing you."

Numbly, Weinglas walked over, climbed in the limo and slammed the door. Only when the limo was halfway down the driveway did Cork and Cathy start laughing hysterically.

Chapter 6

FRIDAY, APRIL 15

Bobby Vangree was still chortling over the reception for Weinglas as he cleared the last Napa stoplight on Highway 29 with only a couple miles to go to Troublante's palace. That poor sucker had been all in when he'd finally gotten on the chartered "crop-duster" at Oak Pass airport to head north. Small planes were best avoided in Bobby's book, and judging from Weinglas' facial expression they were not high on his list either.

Bobby and Brandi enjoyed a good laugh before he'd paid her, and given her an appropriate tip to boot. Great gal, that Brandi, he thought with a smile.

But Weinglas' follies hadn't been the only thing on his mind during his drive up from Oak Pass. He'd been thinking about Laura Troublante. He was convinced she wanted Kildeer Ranch. He just needed to know how far she was willing to go to try and get it. He had to play things cool, tell her he'd pass along her thoughts to the Kildeers, then sit down with Cork and Cathy and figure out what to do.

He wondered what Weinglas would say when he saw him: he knew Weinglas was coming to the reception, as was Smythe and Dudley Samples. That ought to be interesting, he mused.

Oops, here it is, he thought, as he slowed his red rental car and turned through the gate, a massive archway with TROUBLANTE in ornate letters announcing the winery's name. Bobby smiled as he passed under the arch and onto the circular driveway.

Talk about ego, he thought. The building in front of him resembled a huge two-story French chateau – no expense had been spared to achieve an authentic look. The cream-colored exterior was interspersed with tall windows and a steep, gray-tiled roof canted outward at the bottom of the pitch. It was designed in such a way that the front part of the building contained the tasting room on the left as you faced the front entry, with business offices to the right; Laura Troublante's private living quarters were on the second floor.

The driveway encircled a large fountain surrounded by flowers and a broad, green lawn, and brought vehicles to the wide stone courtyard that was large enough to host an outdoor reception for 100 or so people. Smartly trimmed boxwoods bordered the courtyard.

A large parking lot was on the left, so after dropping off passengers at the front door, the driver could continue into the lot; when leaving, the driver would simply turn right back onto the driveway and out the front gate to the highway.

The rear part of the building, easily three-quarters of the total space, was the winery, complete with crush pad, fermenters, barrel room, lab, and case storage.

Drive up to the front in a limo, drive to the back with a truckload of grapes, Bobby thought. The place reeked of decadence.

It was also a hive of activity. Valets were opening car doors and helping people out, then driving off to park. Finally, it was Bobby's turn. He took the claim check and walked across the stone courtyard to one of the biggest, most gaudy residences he'd ever seen.

At the door, a young woman with blond hair in a short bob was sitting at a table, checking guests off a list, and giving them nametags. She smiled and looked expectantly at Vangree.

"Hi, I'm, uh, here for Kildeer Ranch," he said.

The girl had been briefed. Before he could say another word, she said, "Yes, Mr. Kildeer, a pleasure to have you! Welcome to the Napa Valley." She handed him a nametag. It read Hello! My name is Cork Kildeer. "Mrs. Kildeer not with you?"

"Ah ... no," Bobby said.

"Aww," The girl gave a faux pout. "A shame she'll miss the reception. But I'm sure you'll enjoy yourself," she said, motioning him to go inside. Bobby shrugged, put the nametag on and went in. What the hell, he thought, why waste time explaining it to her.

Walking through the massive mahogany doorway, he saw the door to the business offices on the right, a beautiful dark wood staircase ascending to the second floor, and wide French doors opening to the large tasting room and gift shop on the left.

But he was almost knocked over by the sight of a massive portrait on the opposite wall.

It was dark and brooding, featuring an incredible dark-haired woman. She wore a blood-red dress and faced into the wind, which whipped her wild black hair and seemed as if it would tear the dress from her creamy, half-exposed breasts.

It was like one of those romance novel covers, but on a grandiose scale.

It dominated the room and Bobby felt as if the woman's eyes followed him as he walked toward the tasting room. Guess the two-foot name on the gate wasn't enough, he thought.

Entering the tasting room, he was instantly the center of attention. A perfect score from J. Worthington Smythe will do that, especially in the Napa Valley, although Bobby was not sure whether people were happy about it, or resentful. He suspected the latter.

"Hey, Cork, great to see you," a large man in a Brooks Brothers suit said pumping Bobby's hand.

"Great to see you, too!" Bobby said, equally as enthusiastic. This guy's as full of bullshit as I am, he thought.

"How's everything down in Oak Pass?" the guy said.

One of the truisms of the California wine industry is that often vintners from different regions didn't know their colleagues. They might have heard of the wine but never met the person behind it. Clearly, that was what was going on here.

Smythe's review assured that everyone there had suddenly heard of Cork Kildeer, but unless one of them had gone to college with him, it was quite possible, even probable, that no one would know Bobby from Cork.

"Uh, fine, just fine," he said.

"Great review from Smythe," the guy said. "Wouldn't give an old friend a discount would you?" He winked and grinned at Bobby, nudging him with his elbow.

"We can probably work something out," said Bobby, warming to the game. "Gimme a call at the winery. We'll see what we can do."

"Cork, darling," a woman's voice suddenly cooed in his ear. He turned from the mystery man to find a ravishing woman in a revealing cocktail dress.

"Well, hi, darlin'," he said. "How ya been?" He was starting to think this whole situation amusing.

"Not so good," she said, pouting.

"Really? What's wrong?"

"Well, here I see you get a hundred from Smythe, and you don't even call to let me know. But I find out you're going to be up here, and I just know my friend Cork has a case saved for me..."

She tilted her head, giving Bobby her best sultry look.

"Darlin', that's not all I got for you," Bobby said, winking.

"Really?" she said. "Maybe you could get Mr. Smythe to come out to my place? I mean, you're such good friends with him and all. I hear he's going to be here today. And those guys from The Bung."

A nervous pang hit Bobby. While he might be able to bluff by Samples, Smythe and Weinglas were another story. He had to get past this woman now.

"Darlin', you just call anytime," he said, turning to leave. "I'll take personal care of you."

"I'll count on that," she said with a slight tilt of the head and an inviting smile, as Bobby drifted away. I wonder who the hell THAT was, he thought.

A waiter came by, and Bobby took a glass of chardonnay. Time to get to the corner so I can see the whole room, he thought.

Other guests came by, offering congratulations, condolences, advice, and in a couple cases snide remarks. Snobs, Bobby thought.

And then he saw her, looking right at him, those piercing eyes from the portrait seeming to bore right into him. She was wearing a black sleeveless cocktail dress, backless, and gathered in the front, but sufficiently low cut to give a glimpse of her ample charms. Damn, what a woman! Bobby thought as his eyes drifted over Laura Troublante's magnificent body.

She approached him, extending her hand. "Mr. Kildeer, thank you so much for coming. I'm Laura Troublante. I'm so glad you could make it. It's not often someone of your stature drops in." She smiled dazzlingly. Bobby noticed that her grip was firm, confident.

This is weird, he thought, but it might be useful to play the hand out. "Uh, yeah, thanks for the invite," he said. "You have a beautiful house and winery. Very impressive."

"How'd you manage it, the hundred that is?" she asked.

Bobby was taken aback by the suddenness of her advance. "What do you mean?" he said.

"It isn't often that Smythe gives a hundred. It actually happened only once before. So I figure maybe you held his mother for ransom or something like that." She smiled at Bobby, that come-hither look that melted most men.

"Oh, we chaptalize," Bobby said with a mysterious smile of his own, referring to the French practice – illegal in the United States – of adding sugar to the freshly pressed must during the fermentation process to increase alcohol.

She starred at Bobby, not sure whether to believe him, but finally discarded the thought. She laughed, as did Bobby.

"So you do know the process," Bobby said and raised his glass. "Not just a pretty face."

Hmmmm, Laura thought, not what I expected. I thought he'd be a straight arrow, but he looks like he'd actually like to get in my pants.

Hmmmm, Bobby thought, just as I expected. I thought she'd try and throw a curve at me. I wonder if I can get in her pants.

"Cork – you don't mind if I call you that, do you?" Bobby shook his head. "Have you had our wines before?"

"I've had a taste here and there, but no, not really."

"Come with me. I want to hear what you think." She took him by the hand and led him to a tasting bar, where a buff young man was pouring wine. Bobby gave his glass to a passing waiter as they walked.

"Damien, could we start with a chardonnay, please?"

"Of course, Miss Troublante." He set out two wine glasses and poured a couple fingers in each.

"I think this is the wine I was just enjoying," Bobby said, raising his glass in Laura's direction. "Cheers!" She raised hers toward him, and they both sipped. His second glass confirmed his initial thought: a pleasant wine, but unremarkable.

"Unfortunate your wife couldn't be here," Laura said, leaning forward with her elbows on the bar, giving Bobby a full view of her cleavage. He was sure this was no accident. He also realized Laura Troublante had done some homework.

"Where is Mrs. Kildeer this afternoon?"

"She's back at the winery. Just too much happening with the review and all that," he said. "The tasting room's been jammed." All of which was true.

"Ever thought about selling the property?" she said, looking Bobby right in the eye.

Bobby smiled slightly. "No. Kildeer Ranch isn't for sale, Miss Troublante. It's been in the family a long time."

"It's Laura, Cork. I understand the property was purchased for back-taxes back in the '30s," she said.

Bobby nodded, "Yep, that's right."

"Damien, let's try the cab," she said. Damien pulled a cabernet sauvignon from beneath the counter, poured the same amount as before. Bobby sniffed, swirled, and tasted. Not bad, he thought.

"This is a nice wine, Laura. By the way, how would you feel about selling your property here? Everything's for sale for the right price. I was just wondering what yours was."

Laura Troublante just stared at him, not quite believing what she just heard. "Troublante Vineyards is not for sale," she said softly. "Touché."

She hadn't expected he would just walk in and agree to sell to her. She had other avenues to pursue, but his question had made her realize this would not be easy, even though she believed that most men, given a choice, would take the easy road.

Bobby poured the rest of the cabernet in a dump bucket. "What's next?"

"Have you ever tried our late-harvest zinfandel?" she asked. Bobby shook his head. "Damien?"

Damien pulled a beautiful Italian bottle from beneath the counter and poured a small amount in each glass.

Bobby looked at the label. It read, "Troublante Vineyards, 1992, Napa Valley Late Harvest Zinfandel, Alcohol, 15.5 percent by volume."

He sipped: a nice wine, clearly in the dessert category, but with good fruit flavors and a nice spiciness. "Very nice."

Just then, the blonde from the front door came over – her figure wasn't lost on Bobby – and said to Laura, "Excuse me, Miss Troublante, Mr. Smythe just arrived."

"Thank you, Mindy. Cork, would you mind if I greet Mr. Smythe?"

"Not at all," he said, "as long as Mindy can show me around."

"Of course. Mindy, would you mind taking Mr. Kildeer for a short tour?"

"My pleasure," she said, eying Bobby with a mixture of puzzlement and curiosity.

"Laura." He half bowed in her direction, raising his glass. She nodded her head as she moved toward the entrance to greet Smythe. Bobby turned back to his tour guide. "Mindy, shall we?" he said, gesturing in the opposite direction.

"My dear J. Worthington, how wonderful to see you!" Laura said as she extended her hand and leaned over to receive the obligatory air kiss from the great man.

"A pleasure, Laura," Smythe said. "I must say you've put some thought into your place here. Reminds me of some of the places I've seen in France, even more grandiose."

Troublante was slightly irked by Smythe's comment, but knew there was nothing to be done. Shrug it off she thought. Stay on his good side. "Thank you so much," she said. "Would you like to start off with some of our reserve chardonnay, or go straight to the meritage?"

"Some of the chardonnay would be nice," he said. A waiter handed him a glass, and he sipped. "A little heavy-handed on the oak, eh Laura?"

She burned. "Oh, I don't know, J. Worthington. It's a style I think most people like." Then to change the subject: "Did you know Cork Kildeer is here?"

"No I didn't." He looked at Troublante steadily. "I'm guessing you want his vineyard now, don't you? That's why you invited him. Anything to get a better score from me."

Her face flushed at Smythe's impertinence. "Whatever makes you say something like that?"

"Just a hunch. Here, waiter," he got the attention of one passing by, and put his glass on the tray. "Now I'd like to try that meritage." The waiter handed him a glass. He lifted it to his nose and inhaled: a rich, textured wine, he thought.

Just then Troublante said, "Look who's here."

Smythe turned to see, and collided with a tall, slender man whose glasses were knocked off as he got a red-wine bath.

Dudley Samples and Will Weinglas had been arguing all the way to Troublante Vineyards about the Kildeer story. Samples didn't want Smythe to have the satisfaction of knowing The Bung agreed with him. Weinglas insisted the wine was as good as advertised and deserved the cover.

They hadn't settled anything as the valets held their car doors and they alighted at Troublante's.

The smiling young woman gave them their nametags. As they put them on, Samples mumbled, "I hope that fucking Smythe isn't here yet. I really don't want to run into him."

"Me either," Weinglas muttered under his breath.

They walked into the ornate wine palace, and immediately spotted Laura Troublante talking to a man whose back was to them. They walked up their hostess, just as Troublante said, "Look who's here."

The man she'd been talking to turned unexpectedly, accidentally knocking Weinglas's glasses off and spilling red wine all down the front of him.

"Aaaahhhhhh!!!!!" Weinglas yelled. Conversation in the room stopped as all eyes focused on the confrontation. Then, "You!"

"Smythe!" Samples all but hissed.

"Samples," Smythe intoned coldly. "And your lackey Weinglas. Oh, here, sorry about this, but you really shouldn't walk up so suddenly on people. Pardon me, Laura, but I thought this was a reception for professionals." He put his glass on a table, turned and walked away.

"Would you like to see the winery?" Mindy Surlees asked Bobby hopefully.

"Sure," he said, thinking at this point anything to get out of the house, and away fast. Troublante had confirmed what he, Cork and Cathy thought, so no point hanging around to party. But he couldn't just charge past Smythe, plus Samples and Weinglas should arrive any minute. Maybe the best thing would be to stay in the shadows with Mindy.

They walked through a door at the back of a room, which led to a hallway that continued back. Small suites along the hallway were well appointed for guests. At the end of the hallway, Mindy opened another door, and they stepped into the winery.

Oak barrels were stacked five-high, with chalk codes on each head indicating what varietal, lot and vintage were in each.

The room was mammoth. There must have been more than 1,000 barrels stacked in there. They walked into another room, with giant stainless steel tanks running its length.

Bobby's mind was wandering – how do I get out of here – and wasn't paying much attention to Mindy's prattling. If you've seen one barrel, you've seen 'em all, he thought.

Mindy sensed Bobby wasn't paying much attention. "I'm sorry," she said. "I guess this is old hat to you."

"That's OK," Bobby said. "It's interesting to see how someone else does it. We're a pretty small winery. By the way, how long you been here at Troublante?"

"A little over a year," she said.

"You from here or a transplant?"

"Born and grew up here. Went to local schools, then to Sacramento State."

"What'd you major in?"

"Education. I wanted to be a teacher."

"So how'd you wind up here?"

"I got a summer job here between my junior and senior years at Sac, then after I graduated, I got a call from Miss Troublante asking if I would like to come back on a permanent basis. I'm making more than I would teaching, so here I am."

"So what do you do here?"

"A little bit of everything, a Jill of all trades." She laughed.

Bobby smiled. She was nice.

On a table in the dim light, he noticed a case box and a few stray bottles. Underneath the table was another cardboard box with a Del Monte logo on it. Some empty bottles seemed to be in it.

He picked up one of the strays on the table and looked at it. "What's this?" he asked Mindy.

"Oh, that's our port."

"Port?" He looked at the label. The bottle was identical to the late harvest zinfandel he'd tasted just minutes before. The label read, Troublante Vineyards Zinfandel, 1992, 16.5 percent alcohol.

Hmmmm, he thought. A half a percent below the next tax threshold reserved for fortified wines such as port and sherry. Such wines typically have brandy added to fortify them. The average port has 18 percent to 20 percent alcohol, sherry a bit less. So what is this stuff?

"May I try some?" he asked.

"Sure," Mindy said, picking up a corkscrew and pulling the cork. She poured Bobby a taste.

Hmmm, he thought, tastes remarkably like the first one, except a little nuttier. "Where'd you get the brandy for your port?"

"Lucky's," she said, referring to a popular Northern California grocery chain. "Swilly's, Bon Marché, whatever they have." She giggled.

Bobby was dumbfounded. Port was properly made by adding high proof pre-taxed brandy to the still-fermenting wine, which killed the yeast, stopping the fermentation. The resulting wine retained some natural sugar – hence the sweetness – and had a higher alcohol content from the addition of the undiluted brandy, the fortification. But adding commercial brandy straight from the grocer's shelf was a big no-no. And for someone like Laura Troublante, a lawyer who presumably knew the law, to be pulling a stunt like this, well, it boggled the mind. It was risking having the U.S. Treasury Department's Bureau of Alcohol, Tobacco and Firearms, or BATF as it was known, coming in and closing her down if they ever got wind of it.

"Do people buy this?" Bobby asked somewhat incredulously.

"Oh sure," Mindy said. "Women especially seem to like it."

Bobby just shook his head. Then a thought occurred to him. "I'm spending the night in town before going home tomorrow," he said. "Can I talk you into joining me for dinner?"

"Well, I've got to stay 'til the reception's over," Mindy said. "But I guess I could meet you somewhere later."

"How 'bout Relish's, say around 8?"

"Relish's, huh? Pretty upscale." She grinned.

"Nothin' but the best for you, girl!" he said, smiling broadly and bowing slightly.

"OK, it's a date. Mrs. Kildeer won't mind?"

"Nah, she'd understand. Ya see, me and Mrs. Kildeer don't sleep together," he said, winking. "Now, is there a way out back here?"

"Sure," she said. "Follow me."

About 8:20 p.m., Will Weinglas stumbled into Relish's, the popular Napa Valley bistro where the rich and famous frolicked. The place had an outrageously priced wine list to go with its pricey California cuisine which all added up to a gold mine for its owners.

Weinglas was too bummed to care. He was tired of trying to convince Dudley Samples that the Kildeer story was the real news, but he was particularly angry about his run-in with Smythe. What a fucking asshole! All Weinglas wanted right now was a serious buzz, the quicker the better.

He made his way to the bar, not noticing Bobby Vangree and a pretty young woman sitting by the window on the dining room's left; Bobby had asked for a table with privacy in mind for his intelligence gathering.

Weinglas slumped down on a bar stool, and ordered a vodka tonic. He tossed it off, pushed up his glasses, and asked for another. Forget the wine. It had been one of those days.

Bobby saw Weinglas, but observed that he was settling down for a night of self-pity, and decided not to worry about him.

He'd scarcely turned back to Mindy when who should walk in but J. Worthington Smythe, causing a small stir at the front of the restaurant. The maître d' could scarcely contain himself. The great one, the god of all critics, was here! At Relish's! Such an occasion was a serious verification of the restaurant's stature.

Smythe, of course, relished the attention. Completely fawning over him, the maître d' showed Smythe to a table, as luck would have it, within earshot of Weinglas.

Sensing the movement, Weinglas glanced around, saw that it was Smythe, groaned and shook his head. He downed his second vodka tonic and asked for a third. I can't even escape the bastard here, he thought, slumping down farther on his stool.

An aged waiter, gray hair slicked straight back with a slight ducktail, and black horn-rim glasses, approached Smythe and handed him a menu and a wine list. The maitre d' had told the waiter that the patron was a VIP, so be sure to give him the best possible service. The waiter figured that after years of serving Napa's biggest egos he was up to the task.

Bowing slightly, he said, "I apologize, sir, our sommelier is not here this evening. However, I'll do everything I can to help you with your wine selections."

"I'm sure you'll do fine, waiter," Smythe intoned. "Now let's see," he said, flipping open the wine list and scanning down the page. He was silent a few seconds while perusing the list, then said, "I think I'll have a bottle of 1961 Chateau Cos d'Estournel."

Smythe always liked bearding the lion in his own den, so to speak, and ordering French wine in Napa was just that. This was the one local restaurant with a list that allowed him to do it, and selecting a famed *deuxieme cru* was icing on the cake.

"Right away, sir!" the waiter said enthusiastically. Few people ever ordered wines in that price range, and he suddenly anticipated a large tip. Bowing slightly, he headed for the restaurant's wine cellar.

The "cellar" was not actually underground, but was instead a spacious insulated room with separate temperature control containing the restaurant's 21,000 bottles of wine. The waiter opened the door, and stepped in. It was dark in there, and his eyesight wasn't what it once was, and it took a few moments to adjust to the cellar's gloom. But finally he found the Cos d'Estournel bin, far in the back, grabbed a bottle and returned to Smythe. Since Relish's sommelier usually handled the wine selections, it didn't occur to the elderly waiter to check the vintage. That wasn't his gig.

He made a grand show of opening the bottle, and poured Smythe a taste.

Smythe swirled, sniffed and tasted. "That's very good waiter, but that's a '75."

The waiter was startled, as hardly anyone ever rejected a bottle. He wiped the dust from the label, and was astounded to discover that, indeed, he had brought a bottle of 1975 Chateau Cos d'Estournel. "My apologies, sir. Just a minute," he said, and returned to the cellar.

He made straight for the Cos d'Estournel bin, grabbed another bottle, returned to Smythe's table, made the same grand show, and waited. Once again, Smythe swirled, sniffed and tasted. "That's very good, too, waiter, but it's a '66. I asked you for a '61."

The waiter wiped the dust from the label and discovered, to his even greater amazement – and embarrassment – that Smythe was right again.

The maître 'd had noticed that Smythe had rejected a wine – a rare and expensive one at that – and had stepped over nearby to see what was going on. He nearly blew a cork when he saw what was happening.

"My abject apologies, sir. Just a minute," the waiter told Smythe. As he started to turn toward the cellar, the maître 'd grabbed him by the arm and pulled him toward the front counter.

"You fool! You idiot! Don't you know who that is? Here ..." he grabbed a flashlight from the maitre d' stand and shoved it into the waiter's hand. "Make sure you get the right bottle this time!" He was turning red in the face he was so enraged. "Imbecile!"

Weinglas had been sullenly taking this show in, and just shook his head. Anyone else, he might well have been impressed with the ability to discern a wine's different vintages, but he knew that even though the waiter was a bit thick, his bumbling had played right to the wine critic's ego, and that Smythe was now showing off for everyone within earshot. Weinglas almost felt nauseated.

Then an idea began to form in his buzzed haze. He reached behind the bar, grabbed a wine glass, and, turning his back toward Smythe, unzipped his pants and urinated into the large glass, filling it about a third full. He put the 98.6-degree liquid on the bar, and asked the bartender for some ice. He then dumped half the tumbler of ice into the glass of piss, swirling it around to cool it.

Meanwhile, the determined waiter was in the cellar sifting around in the Cos d'Estournel bin; finally, he found the bottle he was looking for. He returned to the table, made the same grand show, poured and waited expectantly.

Again, Smythe swirled, sniffed and tasted. "Ah, '61, just what I wanted," he said. "Thank you, waiter." The condescending tone wasn't lost on Weinglas. That's it, he thought.

"You think you're pretty good," he growled in Smythe's direction, "but I've got a test for you. What's this?" With that, he handed the glass of piss to the bumbling waiter to give to Smythe.

In the darkened room, with the waiter partially blocking his view, Smythe didn't recognize Weinglas. He took the glass, looked at what appeared to be a white wine, and sniffed.

"Yuckh! This smells like piss," he blurted out. Not believing a wine could be that bad, he took a sip. "Bleeaahh!!" he said, spewing the liquid over the table. "It *IS* piss!"

Weinglas had weaved his way over to Smythe. "Damn, you're good," he said. "Now, how old am I?"

Smythe's eyes bulged as he recognized Weinglas, who then turned and staggered out, as Smythe gagged and diners laughed.

Chapter 7

SATURDAY, APRIL 16

Bobby Vangree had enjoyed his drive back to Oak Pass. Mindy had provided some insight into Laura Troublante, plus had proved an energetic lover. A few glasses of wine had loosened her tongue and helped her inhibitions fall away, followed shortly thereafter by her clothes. In fact, she had kept him up most of the night, and he hadn't gotten away from Napa until quite late in the morning.

Troublante, he learned, treated her employees well, as long as they knew their place. But it didn't pay to have an opinion that differed from hers. She was demanding, driven even, but paid well for what she asked. Consequently, she didn't have much turnover.

The more he learned, the more Bobby was convinced that Troublante would pursue Kildeer Ranch relentlessly. He also wondered whether Mindy was part of Troublante's effort to gain leverage; she enjoyed their lovemaking as much as he did, but she also thought she'd been with the married owner of Troublante's target winery, who was apparently estranged from his wife. Would she pass along this bit of information to Troublante, or was the tryst spontaneous? He didn't know.

It was a little before 4 when he pulled into the Kildeer Ranch driveway. The cars were backed up, and the line was still at the plank when he parked in front of the house.

Cork strolled over from the winery and shook his friend's hand.

"Hey, Bobby, how'd it go?"

"I think you have a problem, Cork. A serious problem."

Cork hadn't expected such a frank appraisal, and his heart sank. Bobby saw it on his face.

"Laura Troublante always gets what she wants, and I hate to tell ya, but she wants your vineyard."

"I figured as much," Cork said, turning to see Cathy walking out of the house toward them.

"Hi, guys," she said. "What have you done to my husband that he looks like he just came from a funeral, Bobby?"

"She wants the winery, Cath," Cork said. "Troublante."

"We kinda thought that, babe," she said.

"Cathy, you're about to be dealing with a man-eating piranha," Bobby said. "C'mon inside and I'll tell you what I found out."

Over a glass of wine, he told them of the mix-up, how Mindy had assumed he was Cork, and, since Laura Troublante was none the wiser, she'd believed the nametag. He told of his brief encounter with Troublante, and also of his discovery that Troublante was making a phony port. He also mentioned what he'd heard of the dustup at the reception between Smythe, Samples and Weinglas. And he couldn't help sharing Weinglas' joke on Smythe at Relish's. They all laughed.

"So what do you figure her next move is?" Bobby asked.

"I suspect we'll probably hear from one of her minions or from her directly," Cork said. "Probably won't be long."

About the same time, Laura Troublante was pondering for the fourth time the report she'd asked to be compiled on Cork Kildeer – hometown boy, married to the daughter of a San Francisco scion, well thought of, honest, hard working. She looked at the clipping from the San Francisco Chronicle about Cork and Cathy's wedding. No picture she noted – papers that size rarely ran one. But she did note that Cathy's family, the Phairfields, was well to do, with sufficient connections. That could make things tricky.

She squinted at the wedding photo that appeared in the Oak Pass Tattler. Was that the same guy who was here? she wondered. The picture was coarse, difficult to determine details – and what she was holding was a photocopy. She noted that the Kildeer family had been in the Oak Pass area for decades. She also gleaned that the earlier generation of Kildeers was out of the operation, so not much leverage there.

She looked over the documents from the county courthouse. Everything seemed to be in order, but you never knew. How about contesting the title, she thought. It likely wouldn't go very far, but it would use up some of Kildeers capital, of which she was sure she had a helluva a lot more. She knew a lawyer in that part of the state who would probably file the suit for her. Perhaps an avenue worth pursuing, she thought.

Leverage, leverage, she thought, what I really need is a pressure point. Sex might work – it usually did. She remembered the hungry look she'd gotten from him at her party. He might be married to a cute, busty San Francisco debutante, but he wasn't above fooling around, she thought. Adultery always worked, she smiled to herself.

But she also thought economic hardship might be the ticket. That could be a real persuader. Kildeer

Ranch might be profitable, but until the perfect score it had been a modest operation. How much would it take, she mused, to push it over the edge?

OK, she thought, the ducks are in a row. I'll start with a little gentle persuasion, see where that goes. Then I'll have an idea what to do next.

She found the winery's phone number in the report, picked up the phone and dialed.

Bobby hadn't been gone 10 minutes when the phone rang. "Kildeer Ranch, Cork here."

"Hi, Cork, it's Laura Troublante. How are you? I hope you enjoyed the party."

"You have a great place there, Laura," Cork said, smiling to himself but at the same time a bit stunned by how quickly Troublante was moving. Thank God Bobby arrived back when he did.

"Why, thank you, Cork. How's Cathy doing? Quite a bit of excitement you two have had lately."

"You can say that again. She's fine, busy as hell. So what's up?"

"I'm working with Will Weinglas and Dudley Samples on a feature for The Bung. I don't want to bore you with the details but it's going to be quite a spread – or so they tell me. Of course, I'm sure they'll be wanting to do something on you soon."

"You never know," Cork said. Where was she going with this?

"Well, one of the things I'm trying to do here is create one of the best wineries in the country, and I think Dud and Will recognize that. It's a matter of having the capital to do what has to be done, I'm sure you can appreciate that. But of course, one of the things we need is good vineyards, and I was thinking, what with the rating you just got from J. Worthington that a strategic alliance between Kildeer Ranch and Troublante Vineyards might be something we could talk about."

"I'm flattered, Laura, but I really don't think so. I already have long-term contracts for the grapes we sell, and we're not looking for any new partners."

"I think smart businessmen, people like yourself, always look to see if something might be advantageous to them. An alliance with a winery with our kind of financial clout could certainly help your marketing and distribution. Plus, there might be some other perks."

"I'm not so sure. More than half our business is selling grapes to other wineries, so we don't need a big marketing arm. And the way things have been going these days, we won't have any trouble selling our wine."

"But with your success surely you've thought of reversing those percentages. You can't tell me you haven't thought about it, Cork. What then? You'll need some financial muscle then."

"I don't think so because I haven't thought about reversing those percentages."

"That could be a mistake. You've created demand. How are you going to meet it? Expansion makes sense. And the kind of deal I envision is one where you and Cathy would stay there, run the operation, I'd stay here. Only you'd have the money to do the job right. I think it's a win-win situation."

"Maybe for someone else, but not for us."

"You're saying no, but you haven't even heard an offer. I'm willing to offer a premium. You're obviously worth it. J. Worthington Smythe says so. No one else in this country has gotten a hundred from him. That's worth a lot."

"Tradition is worth more, and ours isn't for sale. It's something you have to earn."

Troublante felt the blood rising to her face. It was a slap. She struggled to maintain control.

"Don't make a decision that you'll regret later," she said, an edge creeping into her voice. "This industry is a small one, and it doesn't help to make enemies. Think about it, that's all I ask. We're talking a comfort level I believe your wife can relate to. Talk it over with her before you make a decision. I think you'll find what I have to offer is more than fair."

"Cathy and I always talk, but it won't change things. We're of one mind on this, Laura, but thanks just the same."

"Just think about it, Cork, and I'll call you in a few days."

Laura hung up and stared at the phone.

"You have to earn it" burned in her ears.

"Fuck you," she whispered at the phone. "Fuck *you*!" she yelled and picked the phone up to throw. She stopped, closed her eyes and set it down. She drew a deep breath and dialed a number.

"Hi, Brent, so glad I caught you, this is Laura, Laura Troublante. ... Yes, it *has* been a long time. Oh, of course I remember the last time. Mmmm. It was for me too." She rolled her eyes as she continued her silky small talk.

Finally, she got down to business. "Listen, Brent, I need a favor. Yes, legal work, sorry, not *that* kind of favor. ... Simple really, for an attorney of your caliber. Yes, a property dispute action. But darling, here's the trick, the client would prefer confidentiality.

"Oh, and Brent, it's a rush job. An extreme rush job. ... I know, I'm sorry. ... OK, how soon could I get it served for triple your normal fee?" She listened for a moment. "Wonderful, Brent! That's excellent! Thank you! I'll have my staff get you the details. ... Yes, yes, I know... I'll be in touch!" She hung up.

Have to earn it, huh? she thought. Maybe you'll be singing a different tune in a few days. A little pinch in the pocketbook will bring you around. More like a sledgehammer. She smiled at the thought of what she was contemplating, which stirred her loins. I haven't had sex in two days, she thought.

She glared at the phone and mashed the intercom button.

"Damien, would you come in here. I have a couple jobs for you."

ZINFORADO!

Chapter 8

MONDAY, APRIL 18

When he thought about it later, Cork realized it was the dog barking that saved them. He and Cathy didn't have one, but the neighbors did. And its incessant barking – what was the time? 1:37 in the morning? – kept hammering at his unconsciousness until it finally got through.

Why is the dog barking like that, Cork thought, as the cobwebs dissipated? Getting up, he walked into the kitchen where he had a view of the winery grounds. Was it his imagination, or was the winery door slightly open? He couldn't be sure in the dark. Better check it out.

He returned to the bedroom, pulled on a pair of Levi's, a sweatshirt, and slipped on a pair of running shoes. Back in the kitchen, he got a heavy duty Maglite 5-Cell D flashlight from the cupboard, then stepped out into the moonlight and walked the short distance to the winery entrance.

The door *was* open. How could that be, he thought? I know I locked it. Better check it out. He opened the door, and instantly realized that something was wrong. A small beam – possibly from a penlight – was dancing among the stainless steel tanks. A metallic noise was audible, then all of a sudden, a splashing sound like someone had turned on a big hose.

But it wasn't a hose. Cork realized that whoever it was had opened the valve on the bottom of one of his stainless steel tanks and was draining it, part of the next vintage waiting to be bottled.

"Hey!!" Cork yelled, flipping on the lights, but they were mercury vapor lights and slow to come on. The penlight immediately went out.

Cork ran to the tank, and frantically started closing the valve, when out of the darkness a fist slammed into his kidney, and he doubled over in pain. A knee met his face as he was bending over, sending him sprawling.

Fighting to remain conscious, blood running from his nose, Cork tried to get up but fell again. Looking in the direction of his attack, he pushed himself up just in time to see a foot streaking toward his head. He rolled quickly and felt the kick graze his hair.

The fog from the initial blows was clearing and as he scrambled to his feet he blindly swung his flashlight toward where he thought the attacker was. He got lucky and struck his assailant's knee. The man grunted at the impact. He tried to step back, but not before Cork, who had pulled himself up, kicked as hard as he could toward the man's groin. He missed what he was aiming for, but hit the tender inside area of the thigh, sending the man staggering backwards, though he didn't go down. But it bought Cork the few seconds he needed to finish closing the valve.

The lights were starting to come on, and Cork could make out through the blood oozing out of his crushed eyebrow and down his face that the man was muscular, probably a body builder, and dressed all in black. He could also tell from the pain that this was no common thug. The man knew exactly what he was doing.

Wary, Cork crouched low as he faced the man. I might die here, he thought, but I'm going down fighting for my family, my winery and my land. He thought it strange that the man just looked at him almost nonchalantly, as if this were just a job.

ZINFORADO!

Suddenly, the man darted through a gap between two steel tanks and raced for the door.

Cork chased after him but was slowed by the pain. He reached the door in time to see a shadow running down his driveway toward the road. The dog was really barking now. Cork ran into the area between the house and the winery, but lost the running man in the darkness. He stood watching toward the road. After about a minute he heard a car start. Headlights flicked on, and in seconds it was gone.

Cork wiped at the blood on his face and discovered he was shaking. His heart was pounding and his kidney hurt like hell. He went back into the winery to survey the damage. The 5,000-gallon tank, one of two, had lost about a quarter of its contents. Even with a headache from a knee to the face, Cork knew that the intruder had cost him thousands.

Who was that? he kept thinking. Whoever it was, he wasn't just some local trying to play a bad joke. The man had known exactly what he was doing, and that by draining Cork's wine Kildeer Ranch would be crippled. It wouldn't have killed them; after all they still sold more than half of what they grew to other vintners. But it would have put him and Cathy in a serious bind.

"Cork?" Cathy's voice was tentative. The mercury vapor lamps were fully lit now and the interior of the winery was awash in light.

"Over here, Cath," he called to her, his back to the door.

She approached him tentatively: "Are you all right?"

He turned to face her, and she gasped. His right eyebrow was smashed, and blood had run down the side of his face; his nose was bloody and still oozing.

"Omigod, Cork! What happened?" she said, rushing up and grabbing his arms, intently looking at his face.

"I heard a dog barking, so I came out to see what was going on," he said. "The door to the winery was open, so I came in and found a guy trying to drain our wine tanks. We got into it, and he ran. He drove off just a couple minutes ago."

"What on earth!" Cathy said. "Why would anyone want to do that? And why would he do this to you? Let's get you cleaned up. C'mon, honey, let's get back to the house and take care of you."

Cathy slipped an arm around Cork's waist, and he winced. "He gave me a shot to the kidney, too," he said. "I think it'll be OK."

They made sure the valve to the tank was firmly closed, then turned out the lights, double-checking to make sure the door was locked as they returned to the house.

Once back in their kitchen, Cathy sat Cork down, found a washcloth and began washing the blood off his face. His nose was sore but not broken – a relief for both of them – and luckily the damage to his eyebrow was superficial. The blow from the knee had split the skin in the eyebrow, which bled profusely, but once cleaned was somewhat hidden by the eyebrow itself.

Satisfied that her husband was more-or-less OK, Cathy looked Cork square in the face, and said, "What is going on here? Why would someone want to drain our tanks?"

"I don't know, Cath, but I gotta tell ya, this guy was no slouch. He was dressed all in black, and looked like he worked out all the time. I've never seen him before. He looked like a pro. But why would anyone want to hire someone to hurt us? He left his car out on the road, I'd guess a couple hundred yards down, near Venturi's driveway. Must have spooked the dog. If that dog hadn't waked me up with his barking, we'd have been in serious trouble."

"I know! How much do you think we lost?

"A thousand, twelve-hundred gallons. I guess we should call the cops and file an insurance claim."

"Yes, we should. How do you suppose he got in there?"

"Good question. I could have sworn I locked that door – I do it every night out of habit. He must have picked the lock – that's the only thing I can think of."

Cathy looked thoughtful for a minute. "OK," she finally said, "we've got a buff guy dressed all in black who parks down the road in the middle of the night who breaks into our winery and tries to drain all our wine. He's clearly intent on doing it, because when you try to stop him, he attacks you. He doesn't run off like someone who's just trying to cause trouble. He tries to put you down. It seems like he runs when he figures he has more to lose by staying. This was planned, babe. Somebody planned this."

"I can't think of anyone around here who would want to hurt us," Cork said, slowly shaking his head. "This has to be connected to the review, but everyone here benefits from us getting that score. It puts Oak Pass on the map."

Cathy dialed the sheriff's office, and told the dispatcher what happened. "I'll get someone out there right away," the dispatcher said.

As they waited for a deputy to come make a report, Cork asked, "You don't suppose Laura Troublante is connected to this, do you?"

"Why do you say that?" Cathy asked.

"I don't know. If it wasn't anybody around here, then who else? She's suddenly become very interested in our property. Word is once she sets her mind on something she'll do anything to get what she wants. I don't know. It's just … after her call a couple days ago, I wonder."

"I've heard that – about her persistence, that is. You may be right, babe."

"Damn!" Cork groaned, leaning down and resting his forehead in his palm. "We ought to talk to Bobby some more about this."

"Here's the deputy; as soon as he's done we're going to get you to the emergency room and get you a couple stitches." Cork started to protest that he'd be OK, but Cathy was having none of it. "Don't even think otherwise," she said.

Cork's head hurt too much to argue. Cheap shot, he thought. I'll remember him.

Damien was thinking much the same thing as he drove north on U.S. 101, back toward Napa. He felt sure he could have bested the man in the winery but that would have taken time, and the man seemed to be fighting to protect home and business. That's a different fight than some blowhard high on testosterone. It was his professional analysis to cut his losses and get out quick.

That damn dog, he kept thinking. Who knew there was a dog there? That bothered him. He had come down early Sunday to get the lay of the land. He'd queued up with the rest of the hoi polloi to taste Kildeer's wine. He'd kept his shades on, was dressed casually, didn't attract attention, wandered with a glass in his hand as if focusing on the wine, and found the two tanks that were the object of his assignment. He had identified the place he wanted to park that night, under an oak tree, out of the moonlight, close enough to get in and out fast. But he hadn't factored in the dog.

He didn't know how much wine had drained out, but he guessed it wasn't enough, and certainly not the two tankfuls he'd planned on.

The other problem was that the man who surprised him in the winery was now alerted and would be on guard; he would also alert others. Laura Troublante would not be happy. Bad luck, he thought, nothing to be done now.

But who was that guy? That wasn't the same guy at the reception a couple weeks ago. So if the guy at the reception was Cork Kildeer, who was the guy in the winery? A worker? A relative of Kildeer's? It puzzled him.

Oh well, he thought, nothing to be done now. The speedometer needle rested just below 90; at this hour, he estimated, with no traffic to speak of, he'd be home a little after sunrise.

Smythe was still smarting from the trick Weinglas had played on him at Relish's. And those damn diners – they'd all laughed. Well, the hell with them, he thought. He'd get even, but just how he wasn't sure. He figured Weinglas had told Samples of his little escapade by now. What a pair. Laugh now, he thought, Laugh now...

His seat in first class was comfortable, and the first-class bubbly he was enjoying was starting to relax him. The flight from San Francisco to La Guardia with a plane change at Chicago O'Hare would get him home by about 10.

He thought about the reception at Laura Troublante's. Her regular wines were OK, nothing to shout about; her reserve wines weren't bad – the meritage, generously, was about a 92, and the reserve cab and chard maybe 90 – but she had clearly wanted him to give her a higher score. Get real. She was a woman who was used to getting her way, and apparently used her mammary glands to manipulate other men. Fools, one and all, he thought, so malleable. That anyone could be so influenced by two glands designed to provide nourishment to infants was stupid.

Clearly, though, they influenced those idiots Samples and Weinglas, because, as he learned at the reception, their next cover story was about Troublante Vineyards. He wondered what angle they'd take, because as best he could tell, she wasn't that interesting: high priced lawyer with questionable scruples decides to get into the wine business. Yawn. That one's been written before. So many more interesting stories abounded in the wine business – hell, Kildeer Ranch was a much better human-interest story.

Then he realized, of course, that it was the advertising. Troublante must be spending a bundle with The Bung. He remembered some years back that a Napa winery was routinely dissed by The Bung, until he, Smythe, had given it a good score – a 98, he recalled – and The Bung was forced to raise its rating.

The Bung guys had come up with some excuses for the initial lowball on that wine, but it must have galled them to dine on crow, especially when the vintner didn't buy any advertising. The shame of it, he smiled to himself.

A flight attendant came down the aisle. "More Champagne for you?" she smiled, extending the bottle in his direction.

What the heck, he thought. "Please." His glass refilled, he took a drink. The effervescence refreshed and relaxed him, helping him refocus his thoughts.

Maybe that was it, he mused. Maybe he could find something connected to the cover story that he could use to discredit The Bung. It would likely also mean discrediting the object of the article. No great loss, he mused.

The rest of his flight was uneventful, and he landed at LaGuardia on time. With only a carry-on bag, he walked straight out to the taxi stand, and was on his way in minutes. At that hour, traffic was light and it took only about 20 minutes to get to his apartment on East 71st Street on the Upper East Side. He was asleep by 11 p.m.

Cork and Cathy got home from Oak Pass Hospital's emergency room about 6 in the morning. As Cork had thought, his injuries weren't serious; as Cathy predicted a couple of stitches had him put back together. Take it easy the next few days, the doctor had told him.

The thought of another day of never-ending phone calls and visitors was almost unbearable. They both longed for the slower pace before the perfect rating.

They lay on top of the bed fully clothed and tried to rest. But Cork couldn't stop replaying the night's events over and over in his mind, and Cathy was still full of adrenaline, and by 8 o'clock they gave up. They decided to call Bobby and see if he could make any sense out of the night's happenings, but before they could Bobby showed up with three extra-large coffees from a local coffee shop.

"So you had an early morning visitor," he said once they'd settled around the table in the Kildeers' kitchen.

"How'd you hear about that?" Cork asked. "That was only, let's see … six hours ago."

"It's a small town, Cork. The dispatcher called a friend, who told a friend, who was in line at the Coffee Hut; then the emergency room nurse got into the act. I figure by now the whole town knows that you were attacked."

Cork and Cathy looked at each other and shrugged. "You're probably right," Cork said in a resigned tone. Then: "Who would do this to us, Bobby? Is there someone around here who secretly hates us? Have we pissed somebody off?"

"Whoa, Cork, slow down; tell me what happened first," Bobby said.

Cork told how the barking dog had waked him, how he had surprised a muscular man clad in black in the winery, how if it weren't for the barking dog, they wouldn't have had any wine to sell after the current release was gone.

"My hunch is it wasn't anyone locally, but I'm just not sure," he told Bobby. "I mean, most people here celebrate their neighbors' successes because ultimately it means more business for them. This guy looked like a hired gun."

Bobby sipped his coffee and looked at Cork.

"If this guy was a pro, have you asked yourself, who could afford a hit man, and why would they bother? I don't think it was locals either." He sipped again. "So why do I think Laura Troublante had something to do with this?"

Cork took a sip. "I gotta tell ya, I had the same thought."

They all sipped and looked at each other.

"Wait a minute guys, let's step back a second," Cathy said. "We've had one conversation with her on the telephone. OK, yeah, she wants our vineyard, but it's hard for me to believe that after one phone conversation she'd resort to breaking and entering ... and sabotage. She's a businesswoman, not a thug."

"She thinks she's met you, though," Bobby said, looking at Cork. "And she asked where Mrs. Kildeer was when I met her. So look at her history. When she does something, typically she moves fast. When I was at her reception, one of the first things she asked was about selling. She also asked if the ranch had been bought for back taxes. Lawyers usually don't ask questions they don't know the answer to. Clearly she'd done some research and had been thinking about this. That was just the first volley.

"So then she pushes a little harder. She calls you up and wants to buy; now it's not just party conversation that could be taken lightly. Now she's played one of her face cards. I think she was trying to find a pressure point, push and see what happens."

"OK, what you're saying makes sense, but I still don't understand why," Cathy said. "I get it that she may be envious of the score Smythe gave us, but to suddenly want our land? It's like, Travis Ellis just bought a new car, and I think it's a really great car, but I don't want to take it from him."

"I've been thinking about that, too," Bobby mused. "I just met her that one time, so all I really know about her is what I've heard and read. And what I've read makes me think she's almost a sociopath – she goes around gobbling up what she wants and doesn't care how she treats people. The wine biz is too small to keep that up for long."

He paused for a sip of coffee, then continued: "There were some rumors about her going around a few years back, when she was just getting into the wine biz, about some court case she was involved in. She had a conference in the judge's chambers, and awhile later the judge issues a favorable ruling. There was speculation about what might have gone on during that meeting; perhaps it was just coincidence. Who knows? But the smart money says she either sucked him or fucked him."

Cork looked at Cathy, and she back at him, and they both started giggling at his coarse characterizations. Bobby smirked and seemed pleased that he'd put a smile on their troubled faces.

"Here's something else: I tasted her wines while I was there, and they're just OK, commercial-grade wine. The high-end stuff's not bad, but the regular bottlings are ordinary at best. Whatever she's doing there isn't cutting it. She's built this gaudy showpiece of a winery, and the wines don't match it. I think she knows it and wants your vineyard to prop up the image she's bought herself."

"So all this, the hard sell and maybe even hiring a hit man ... it's all for ego?" Cathy asked.

Bobby shrugged.

"By the way, Cork, what did this guy you surprised look like?"

"About 6-feet or so, built like a linebacker. Short dark hair."

"Laura Troublante has a guy like that working for her. He was pouring wine when I was there. Quiet, didn't say much, but I'm betting he wasn't hired for his wine-pouring prowess."

"You're kidding. You saw this guy at the reception?"

"Well, somebody who sounds just like him. I suspect Troublante's behind this, so I wouldn't be surprised if it's the same guy. If it was, my guess is she sent him down here to dump your wine down the drain. I'm thinking that she's thinking that with nothing to sell, you might want to play ball with her."

Cork shut his eyes, put his head down and started rubbing his temples. "I just wanted to make some good wine," he mumbled to no one in particular. Cathy put her arm around his shoulder and gently hugged him, then kissed the top of his head. Bobby studied his feet.

Cork took a deep breath and let it out. "Tell you what," he said. "I've got to get a locksmith out here to see what we can do to better secure the place; if that guy got in once, I don't want him coming back to finish the job. And I've got to lie down for a bit; my head is really hurting. Whaddya say we all meet about 1 at Boobsie's to talk about this some more, and see if we can't get TR to join us. He's been in the business a lot longer than either of us and may have some insights."

"Deal," said Bobby, leaping up. "That's one of my favorite places. I'll call TR, you guys worry about what you need to do here. See you about 1." He tossed his paper coffee cup in the trash, and with a smile and a wave strode out to his truck and headed out.

Watching Bobby go, Cork asked, "What have we gotten ourselves into, Cath? What have I gotten you into?"

"Quit that," she said, quietly but firmly. "We're in this together – thick 'n' thin, remember? So maybe this is one of those thin times, but it'll all work out.

"Now I'm going to call a locksmith, and you're going to lie down – don't argue with me, babe!"

Cork had opened his mouth as if to protest. He looked at her for a couple seconds, then shifted his gaze and nodded. He slowly got up, wandered into their bedroom and lay down. He knew he would only get light sleep at best, but the simple act of resting would help.

Cathy was slightly embarrassed by the naiveté of their security. The winery doors themselves were solid – insulated metal doors in metal frames. But while the locks were a popular brand, they were simple doorknob style locks. A deterrent to most honest people, the locks would probably not offer much resistance to someone determined to break in.

The locksmith she had called examined the locks on the front and back doors, and had not been able find any damage, which meant, as Cork suspected, the intruder had used a tool to pick the lock. The locksmith recommended a double-cylinder deadbolt be installed, and strongly suggested that the Kildeers consult a security service about installing a burglar alarm.

Cathy asked the locksmith to install the recommended deadbolts; it would take a bit of doing since the doors were metal, but he had the right tools for the job. As he began his work, she wandered into the winery to look around and think. She picked up a hose and began washing down the concrete where the wine had spilled, the spray pushing everything into the floor drains.

What do we know about this Troublante woman? she thought. She's rich: made a lot of money as a lawyer. She's powerful: made a lot of friends – or at least acquaintances – along the way. She's ruthless: lets nothing stand in the way of what she wants. Was she a sociopath, like Bobby thought? Perhaps dissocial. From what little Cathy had heard, the woman had little regard for others' feelings; empathy was not in her vocabulary.

Finishing the cleanup, she looked at her watch: a quarter to 10. The tasting room opened at 11, and the two college kids who manned the "tasting plank" would be here in about an hour. She hoped Cork could rest at least until then.

Her thoughts returned to Troublante. She smiled at Bobby's speculation of how Troublante had gotten a favorable court ruling. If there was any truth to the rumors at all, it indicated that sex was another "face card" for Troublante, as Bobby would say. It was especially effective on men; and you didn't have to actually play that face card to be effective. The ace could be saved for something you really wanted.

Cathy knew a little of that game. As a teenager just beginning to explore her own sexuality, she had tantalized a high-school classmate, just to see what his reaction would be. Of course he was smitten. She had to cease the charade and tell him she really wasn't interested. He had been hurt, and she was ashamed of her behavior. That was not what she was about. But she also learned from the experience, and instinctively understood the power she possessed and how powerful sex was in manipulation.

Regardless of Troublante's schemes, Cathy knew Cork loved her with every ounce of his being, that she was precious to him. No one else mattered, nothing else tempted him. She loved him that much, too.

It slowly occurred to her that she would likely be playing a much bigger role in what was to unfold. At the moment, she didn't know what that would be. She was looking forward to lunch and wanted to hear what Travis Ellis thought, see if he knew anything more about Troublante, provide any answers.

She checked on the locksmith and found that he was an efficient fellow and had already finished one door and was nearing completion on the second one. A few minutes later he was done. He gave Cathy the new set of keys, told her he would send them a bill, and left.

Cork and Cathy pulled into the parking lot at The Boobsie Twins – known locally as Boobsie's – at five 'til 1. Much of the lunch crowd had dissipated, and Cork and Cathy were able to secure a large corner booth.

Boobsie's was home to great burgers – none finer on the Central Coast – and was popular with locals and visitors alike. Its owner, Millie Bounty, understood the value of meeting friends in low places, and that good burgers were universal currency.

Millie was aptly named; a bounteous, buxom woman, she had been an active participant in the '60s social upheaval, and had been around far more blocks than she could remember. Married and divorced a couple times, she'd exited life's fast lane at the Oak Pass off-ramp in hopes of finding one of life's country roads. It was exactly what she was looking for.

She'd found a vacant old brick building in downtown Oak Pass that had been on the market for who knew how long, and bought it for a song. She'd spruced it up, installed a kitchen, and, with a twinkle in her eye, applied the name she'd given her own ample pillows. The place had been a hit since the day it opened.

She had a motherly quality, a worldly wisdom that just naturally drew people to her. She genuinely liked people, and made every effort to ensure they had a good experience at Boobsie's. She hired young women as servers – mostly from the college a half-hour down the road – for two reasons: she wanted to provide opportunities for women trying to get ahead, and hey! honey attracted far more customers than vinegar.

She maintained a good working environment where the "girls" felt safe, and the tips were great. She was aware that the combination of boobs and boys had its risks, but testosterone-fueled discussions were never tolerated at Boobsie's. You did not want to be confronted by an angry Millie Bounty. Misbehave in her establishment, and you'd find yourself out on your ear, tossed personally by the owner herself. She'd had to do that a couple times when she first opened, and the word spread fast: keep your hands to yourself, and be respectful of the staff. She took good care of both her customers and her employees.

Millie was also one of the most generous people in the community. She had a desk drawer full of school-fundraiser raffle tickets that she'd bought over the years, and must have equipped the entire high school band from all the chocolate bars she'd bought (she always gave the candy to the kid selling it). She gave regularly to local charities, and often provided free meals to unfortunates. She was an active member in the local chamber of commerce, and was a past president of the Oak Pass Rotary Club.

Ironically, Millie Bounty, the ex-hippie, freewheeling, anything-goes gal, had become a beloved local institution, part of the establishment.

She saw Cork and Cathy come in and ambled over with a big smile and a hearty, "Hi guys, great to see you! You two are looking great!" She pointedly made no reference to Cork's stitched-up eyebrow.

"Hi Millie," Cork responded. "Wish we felt great. I suppose you heard we had a bit of trouble last night."

"I did hear something about that, but the important thing is you're here, and we're going to take good care of you. What can I get you to drink? You waiting for someone?"

"Yeah, TR and Bobby are joining us; they oughta be here any time now. Uh, diet soda – whichever – is fine for me."

"Same for me," Cathy said.

"You got it, kids, then I'll have Kelly look after you."

Millie turned to leave just as Bobby Vangree and Travis Ellis walked in. "Sheesh, Millie, you'll let anyone in this joint," said Travis, winking at Cork and Cathy, and bending down to give Millie a peck on the cheek.

"Well, I let you in, didn't I?" she said, grinning. They all chuckled at the good-natured ribbing. "What'll you guys have to drink?"

"Water for me," Travis said.

"Diet here," from Bobby.

"Coming right up," and off she went.

Travis Robert Ellis, known to close friends as TR, was a burly fellow, considered the local godfather of vintners. Born and raised in Oak Pass, he'd become interested in wine making after he took an introductory wine appreciation course at Fresno State. He didn't hear the snickers from classmates when he'd ask why is this wine red and this wine white. But the professor didn't snicker and patiently explained how the skins make the color, while the soil makes the flavor.

The more he learned the more Travis wanted to learn. The wine bug had bitten him. He quickly changed majors and graduated with honors with a degree in enology and viticulture. He got a job at a large vineyard an hour or so north of his hometown. The vineyard sold most of its grapes to other wineries, but used a small amount for its own label. It was an ideal spot to gain experience. But after three years he wanted to go home.

His education and experience convinced him that Oak Pass would be a great place to grow grapes, but at that time there were only a few vineyards there, Kildeer Ranch being one of them. His parents grew walnuts and almonds, and he managed to convince them that grapes were the wave of Oak Pass's future. They tore out some old almond trees that were going to have to come out anyway, and planted 20 acres of cabernet sauvignon.

Travis commuted to his job at the big vineyard to the north for a couple years while tending to the new vines at his parents'. He returned to his family venture full-time at the third-leaf, when the new grapevines first produced a crop. The resulting wines were well received, and the Ellises expanded their vineyard. Now, some 35 years later, Travis had 500 acres of vines, truckloads of medals from various wine competitions, and the well-deserved respect of his peers. He served on statewide industry committees and boards, and was well connected up and down the state.

If anyone would have insights into Laura Troublante's motives, it was Travis Ellis.

After their beverages had arrived, and Kelly had taken their orders, Travis said, "So Bobby tells me there's trouble in paradise. What's going on with you two?"

Cork looked at Cathy, then at Travis. "What can you tell us about Laura Troublante?"

"Laura? Oh, she's just your everyday, garden-variety great white shark. If you're looking for someone to eat you alive, she's a good bet. Why? How'd you get involved with her?"

"Not by choice," Cathy said. "It's like she's suddenly targeted us."

"Tell me what happened."

They related what had occurred since getting the 100 points from Smythe, the invitation to Troublante's reception, the mix-up with Bobby, the call from Troublante, and the late-night visit from the man in black who might be a Troublante henchman.

As they were finishing the story, their burgers arrived, and a couple minutes passed as they all mmmm'd and ahhh'd over the great flavors.

Finally, Travis said, "Here's the deal on Laura Troublante. She's made it well known in wine circles that she wants a 100-point wine. She got into the business because she wanted a place to spend her money, where she could be at the top of the social heap. She really doesn't know the first thing about the wine business, only what she reads in The Bung, Smythe and other publications like that. But she knows how to spend money on quality grapes and quality people to do the work for her. And spends a lot of money.

"I'm betting it bugs the hell out of her that you came along, seemingly out of nowhere, and took that Numero Uno position she's been shelling out so much money on.

"She built this huge winery in Napa because she wants to be the center of attention. She wants to be the number-one destination in Napa. But it gets back to not knowing the business. She doesn't really understand that wine is a dirt-under-the-fingernails business, that it takes work and commitment. She wants it all now without earning it.

"She figures she can buy her 100-point wine from you. And if you aren't willing to go along with what she wants, she'll figure out a way to get you to go along."

"OK, but I told her I wouldn't sell," Cork said.

"From what I've heard, that doesn't usually stop her," Travis said. "She'll up her price. Or add something else you want more than money."

He looked pointedly at Cork who replied, "Yeah, I've heard about her bedroom negotiations, and that sure as hell isn't happening."

Cathy grabbed his hand under the table and Cork kissed his wife's shoulder.

"Ok, lovebirds," Bobby said through a mouthful of fries.

Travis washed another bite of burger down with his water, and wiped his mouth. "Well, if we really think Laura sent that guy last night, and frankly, it seems a little far-fetched to me, then it's about hitting you where it would hurt, your cash flow. She probably figures that's your weak spot. No wine, no money, no way to tell her no. She analyzes all the angles. Dump your wine down the drain, and you'll have to sell to her. That would be my guess."

"Have you met her?" Cork asked.

"Couple o' times," Travis responded. "The first time was an industry confab up in the capital a couple years back; she was there. Looked like she was sizing up the fish. The governor was the keynoter, and since he and I went to college together, I was seated at the head table next to him. He wasn't there yet when I introduced myself to her. She seemed pleasant enough, but I got the impression she wasn't interested in me as a person, just how I could advance her ambitions. I didn't have anything she wanted so she looked through me, barely shook my hand. But when the governor showed up and she saw we were buds, she suddenly turned on the charm. That's Laura Troublante."

Bobby nodded. "Sounds about right," he said.

"But why do you think it's far fetched about that guy last night?" Cork asked.

"Because Laura Troublante may be a user and all ego, but she's also a businesswoman, not some arch assassin out of a novel," Travis replied. "And remember, she's a lawyer. Whatever her shortcomings, the woman is sharp, from everything I've heard."

"Sharp?" Bobby snorted. "Then why's she fooling around with fake port?"

"Fake port?" Travis raised an eyebrow.

"Yeah, she's putting some stuff out that's blended with brandy straight from the supermarket."

Travis looked at Bobby for a couple seconds. "Are you shittin' me? Where'd you hear that?"

"From one of her people, gal named Mindy. I even tasted the stuff. Actually wasn't bad."

Travis put his forehead in his right hand, and shook his head in disbelief. "Wow! Hard to believe that someone with her background would pull a stunt like that."

"I dunno, TR," Bobby said. "If she's like you say, so all-fired up to get ahead and be the top place in Napa, no telling what she might do."

"Well, if you're looking for a weak-spot, I think you just found one," Travis said.

"How so?" Cathy asked.

"What she's doing is highly illegal," Travis said. "It's a taxation issue. Port has a higher alcohol content than table wine, which puts it in a higher tax bracket. So she's essentially selling spirits but paying taxes on wine. The government's not getting its share. And the government doesn't take well to that. If the BATF got wind of it, they'd close her down in a flash."

"They could do that?" Cathy asked. "Just close her down?"

"Oh, you better believe it," Travis said. "In order to get your BATF bond – and you can't operate a winery without it – you basically give away your rights to just about everything having to do with the business. The feds can come in, ask whatever they want, look at whatever they want, do whatever they want."

"But don't you need a search warrant or something?" asked Cathy.

"Nope. The feds have carte blanche." Travis took another bite of burger, then continued. "A couple years ago a woman agent showed up at my place for a spot inspection. She asked to look at some of my records. I said, 'Can you give me an hour or so? The tasting room's really busy.' She said, 'Mr. Ellis, you can either get me those records now, or I'll run all those people out of your tasting room and slap a padlock on your front door so fast it'll make your head spin. Now what's it gonna be?' I said, 'What were those records again?' That's the kind of power I'm talking about."

"Wow." Cathy shook her head.

"I guess we haven't had our turn in the barrel with the BATF, at least not yet," Cork said.

"Suppose," Bobby mused, "that the BATF showed up at Troublante's wanting to see the records for that port. What do you think she'd do?"

"Either fuck 'em – sorry, Cathy – or talk her way out of any trouble. Believe me, she does whatever it takes."

"What kind of record-keeping's involved for port?" Cathy asked.

"You have to have fortification records, showing exactly what and how much you added to your wine. If she's just adding stuff from the supermarket, I doubt she has any fortification records. Bobby, did the label say it was port?"

"Nope, just said it was zinfandel, 16-and-a-half percent alcohol. But they're telling people it's port."

Travis just shook his head, amazed that someone with a legal background would take such a risk.

"Port that's not labeled port," Cork thought out loud. "So technically she doesn't have to have fortification records. You think she's just making money on a loophole? Why would anyone mess around with something like that?"

"I don't know," Travis said. "It's such a risk. Someone, like Bobby's little friend Mindy, might talk. Or if someone ever got a hold of the stuff it could be tested and the feds would be all over her."

Cork was beginning to see how diabolical Laura Troublante was. Like Travis, he couldn't figure out why Troublante would be fooling around with something that could cost her dearly. But it might just be the edge they needed. An idea began forming.

"Suppose we could get our hands on a bottle of that stuff," he wondered. "Would there be any way we could tell that the brandy wasn't the right kind, that it was over-the-counter brandy?"

"Yes," Travis said. "You could use a high-performance liquid chromatograph, or you could use a gas chromatograph mass spectrometer, which would tell you about the oak that the brandy was aged in. The tests are pretty costly, but you could do it."

Cork popped the last bite of burger into his mouth and chewed silently for several seconds. We've got to get our hands on one of those bottles, he thought. He looked at his wife, who returned his stare.

"Suppose," he said softly, "a couple of BATF agents showed up at Troublante's looking for fortification records and a sample of that wine."

"Well, good luck with that," Travis said, enjoying the last of his French fries.

"So are you thinking of just going down to the BATF and saying, 'Hey, better check this place out 'cause they got a phony port?'" Bobby asked. "I'm not sure they'd bite."

"They might, but I wouldn't have much on her if they did. No, we have to get a hold of one of those bottles."

Travis stared at him, incredulous.

"As in, impersonate a BATF agent and scare it out of her?"

"Well, when you say it like that..."

"Cork," Travis said waving his hands. "I know you got knocked around last night, but..."

"Or we could just buy a bottle," Cathy added.

"I don't think so," Bobby said. "Mindy told me it's only available to their wine club members, and isn't even in the tasting room. It's a special deal for friends of the winery, people Troublante trusts. Asking about it could sound an alarm."

They were all quiet a minute.

Travis started to get nervous.

"Seriously, guys, you can't..."

"Hiya! You Cork Kildeer?" a young man in jeans with a plaid, short-sleeved shirt and loosened tie stood leaning over the table expectantly.

"Uh, yeah, what's...?"

"Great!" the man said and handed Cork a manila envelope. "You've been served!"

And he walked jauntily out the door.

Cork was dumbfounded as he opened the envelope and read the contents.

"Lawsuit," he mumbled.

He crumpled the page and looked at Travis.

"A San Francisco family trust is claiming it's the rightful owner of Kildeer Ranch," he said.

"What?" "You've got to be kidding..." "That can't be!" they all exclaimed simultaneously.

Cathy took the paper and began reading feverishly.

"What family trust?" Travis asked. "What's the name?"

"Acme," Cork answered.

"What the hell kind of name is that?" Bobby asked.

"The kind that means you don't want anyone to know who you really are," Cathy said looking up from the papers.

"Still think Troublante isn't behind all this?" Cork asked Travis.

Chapter 9

TUESDAY, APRIL 19

J. Worthington Smythe gazed out across the canyons of Manhattan from his 39th floor office and pondered how to get even with Samples and Weinglas.

His anger at being duped into tasting urine was still palpable. Holding court for the benefit of the stupid waiter and the hoi polloi within earshot was just showing off, he had to concede. But that was his shtick: he had a gift for evaluating and identifying wines.

That buffoon Weinglas wasn't even in the same league! He wouldn't dare pull a stunt like that sober. How dare he humiliate the great Smythe! But that's exactly what he had done.

It occurred to Smythe, as he sat there, that any journal is only as good as its credibility, that without credibility it's only the Weekly World News. What an odd collection of nonsense that rag was. Surprisingly, he thought, some people actually believed its drivel. At a party one time some matron had assured him that Elvis really did communicate from the spirit world with creatures from outer space. She knew it was true because she had read it in the Weekly World News.

Smythe shook his head at the memory. Humph, he thought, The Bung wasn't much better: everyone knew all you had to do to get a good review or story was buy an ad, despite Samples' protestations to the contrary. But essentially those reviews were editorials; they were the opinions of Samples or Weinglas or whoever evaluated the wine. Essentially, Smythe admitted to himself, they were no less valid than his own observations.

But stories were different. There should at least be a germ of truth, some accuracy in a feature. Could he discredit the Troublante Vineyards cover story The Bung had scheduled? He took another swig of coffee. He had thought about it on the plane. He didn't know what the story would say, but could guess that it would be the usual fluff about the glorious new temple to wine, and how happy Troublante was to be part of the wine community, blah, blah, blah.

He thought about how Laura Troublante had managed to get a Bung cover story in the first place. He had noticed that the previous few issues had full-page color ads touting her winery. Those weren't cheap; she'd obviously spent a bundle at The Bung. What if she stopped buying ads? What then? Would Samples care? On balance, Smythe thought Samples would.

In fact, the more he thought about it, it seemed to him that ad revenue was Samples' and Weinglas' Achilles heel. Samples was a businessman: advertising revenue was what he focused on. Weinglas was the content guy. If advertisers thought the content attracted readers, they would keep advertising. But if advertisers got the idea that their ads weren't working, or the magazine wasn't reaching the right audience or that the magazine was not living up to its promises, they likely would stop advertising. That would cause acrimony all around.

Clearly The Bung's audience was the right one for any winery, and Smythe was confident that the ads were produced by an agency that worked closely with Troublante. That left the question of the magazine living up to its promises. And the promise had been the cover story.

Suppose Samples got the idea that Troublante was about to pull her advertising. That ought to get him stirred up. And if Samples got the idea that her unhappiness was somehow connected to the cover story, he'd have Weinglas out there quick. Or suppose Troublante got the idea that Samples and Weinglas were playing fast and loose with her. The threat that she might haul The Bung into court would make those two dolts shit their pants. He laughed out loud at the thought.

His assistant came into his office at the sound. "Did you need something, Mr. Smythe?" she said.

He was still chuckling to himself. "No, Josephine, not just yet. But I'll have something for you shortly."

Josephine would have been better off being named Jane, Smythe thought, as in plain. But her appearance was of no concern to him. In fact, he could care less. She was efficient, loyal, and had an excellent palate in her own right. She also shared his disdain for The Bung.

His plan was forming slowly; how best to implement it?

Cork and Cathy were bracing for another day of mega sales. It had only been a week since Wines by Smythe had anointed Kildeer Ranch's zinfandel as the greatest North American wine ever. And even following Bobby's advice and jacking up the price to $50 a bottle hadn't slowed sales at all. In just a week they'd sold half of the now famous zin.

Cork was scrambling some eggs when Cathy came into the kitchen. It only had been a little more than a day since he'd thwarted the man in black from crippling their young winery, and he still had some aches as a result of the encounter.

Then that lawsuit! Luckily, Travis's brother, a lawyer, had offered to look into it for a reduced rate. On the surface, Cork thought it was bogus. Even so, it would cost them something to get it thrown out.

Both incidents, though, had galvanized Cork. Cathy saw the fire in his eye, and knew he would do everything he could to defend their home and livelihood. That told her they were going on the offensive. The football player in Cork was ready for the second half.

While Cork finished plating the eggs and a couple sausage links each, she buttered some toasted English muffins and added them to their plates, poured a couple glasses of orange juice, and the two of them sat at their kitchen table.

"I've got an idea," Cork said as he lifted a forkful of eggs.

"I kinda picked up on that at Boobsie's," she said. "Why do I think it has something to do with a couple of BATF agents asking Laura Troublante for her fortification records and a sample of her so-called port."

Cork smiled at his wife. "You got it, babe. And the best part is that you and I are going to be the BATF agents."

"What!?! You're not serious!"

"You bet I am!"

Before she could say any more, Cork rushed on. "Look, she doesn't know me or you from Adam and Eve. She thinks Bobby's me. And you heard TR, BATF agents get what they want, no questions asked. We go to her winery, ask to see her records and get a bottle of the 'port.' She won't have any reason to doubt we're who we say we are. Once we have that bottle we have a bargaining chip. Like TR said, that's her weak point."

Cathy stared at him.

"Babe, I can't just sit here and wait for her next attack!" The exasperation was rising in his voice. "This is our land, our home we're talking about. We need to do something. And no way will she be expecting it."

Emotionally spent, he sat waiting for Cathy to say something.

She just stared at him.

Cork stared back. The incongruity of his plan began to seep into his consciousness. This is nuts. Impersonate federal agents? TR was right. It sounds absurd after I said it out loud. What was I thinking?

"Uh ... wow," Cathy finally said.

"Yeah, maybe you're right," Cork interjected, dejectedly. "I don't know what..."

"I wonder if we could pull it off."

Cork stopped and watched his wife as her creative mind went to work.

"We'll need some kind of identification. She's a lawyer so she'll want to see that. And we need to make sure she's there so we don't get some employee who's more afraid of her than the BATF."

Was Cathy really on board?!? Suddenly Cork's urgency returned.

"Yeah, I thought of that. We could call Thursday afternoon to make sure she'll be there Friday. We'll tell her that two agents will be there Friday around 11 o'clock to check records. We don't want to alarm her too much, but to make sure she's there when we arrive. We'll confiscate – quote-unquote – a bottle of that fake port, and head back here as fast as we can."

"Friday?" Cathy said. "You want to do it this Friday?"

"Yeah, because I don't think she'll be expecting us to do anything, especially not that soon. From what we've heard, she's never had to deal with a counter-attack, so that's just what we'll do."

Cathy looked thoughtful. "Hmmm. ... Yeah. ... Friday will work." She paused for a few seconds. "We can get TR or Millie to call and let her staff know two agents are headed her way. And we'll ask Bobby or TR to help us with the IDs. You're right, it has to be quick, because Lord knows what else she has planned." She took a bite of English muffin.

She *was* in! This could really happen! Cork realized he was staring at her with his mouth open. He snapped it shut. Cathy glanced over at him and asked, "What? Why are you looking at me that way?"

"Uh, nothing. I just thought you were going to try and talk me out of this crazy stunt."

Cathy smiled. "I think with this lady, crazy is about the best plan we have."

"So you're OK with impersonating a couple BATF agents? I mean this is deep shit, Cath."

"Well, as you pointed out, we're already in deep shit. The more I think about it the more I like it. And honestly, I don't see a better option. Besides, it's not like she's going to call the cops on us when she has a winery full of illegal 'port.' No, with her, I think our biggest concern is the bluff."

She took a swig of coffee and continued: "We have to do this right. We already know that with her, it's all offense, no defense. If she can't bully you, she buys you. If she can't buy you, she seduces you. She's not stupid enough to try and bully or buy federal agents, so she's down to seduction. She'll think it's two guys. She'll think she can handle them with sex – flash some boob, give a few flirty answers and voila! the feds'll forget why they even came.

"But a female agent, the lead agent – *that* she won't have any game plan for. Especially an agent like the one who hit TR."

She looked at Cork with a faint smile. He recognized the brilliance of her scheme.

"Wow!" he laughed and reached for her hand. "Who the hell did I marry?"

"Someone who's with you no matter what," Cathy said, beaming.

"I never had the slightest doubt," he said.

Impulsively he leaned forward and kissed her. She grabbed the back of his head and held their kiss for several seconds.

They were in this together.

Damien was right. Laura Troublante wasn't happy with his report. But Laura hadn't reached her stature in life by reacting emotionally. She'd expended some bile in Damien's direction, but agreed with his assessment: cut your losses and get out. It made no sense whatsoever to maim or possibly even kill whoever it was that discovered Damien. The complications from such a scenario would have made it far more difficult for her to accomplish her goal, which was to acquire Kildeer Ranch. The barking dog was just bad luck, she mused. Otherwise young Mr. Kildeer may have been facing an economic loss that would have led to his capitulation much sooner.

So what now? Cork Kildeer had been blunt on the phone: the property was not for sale.

The lawsuit she'd had filed claiming a family trust had prior interest in the property was a sure loser, she knew. Winning wasn't the point. The point was to bleed Kildeer over time and drain him of funds.

The problem with this tack, she thought, was time. Lawsuits could drag on. And while that was sure to deplete Kildeers reserves – assuming he had much –

before it even dented hers, she was impatient to get that vineyard.

She tapped her fingernails on the varnished hardwood of her desk. Let the lawsuit play out while I find another crack in the Kildeer armor, she figured. She let out a heavy breath.

It's too bad that Kildeer was proving such a tough nut to crack, she thought: Why is he being so obstinate? He was standing in my own tasting room, chatting with me, tasting my wine, looking down the front of my dress and mentally undressing me. It was the perfect setup. Men are so easy to read; I know that look. And he's married! Even more leverage. I would fuck his balls blue if it meant getting my hands on that vineyard. Most men would jump at the chance to get me in bed, and I thought he was ready to jump – married or not. But talking to him on the phone, it was like we'd never met, polite but no sense of recognition. It was like he was two different people.

Chapter 10

WEDNESDAY, APRIL 20

Will Weinglas enjoyed wine competitions. It was a chance to see colleagues, catch up on industry gossip, taste wines – some good, some bad – get some story ideas. The judges' dinners were always fun, and a good way to forget about life's knotty issues, like that prick Smythe.

The Palm Springs International Wine Competition was one he particularly looked forward to. It was a three-day affair, with the judging rounds Wednesday and Thursday, and the sweepstakes round on Friday. He should be done by about 3 p.m. Friday, in plenty of time to catch a flight back to Chicago out of Ontario.

Weinglas had waked late Saturday morning in his Napa hotel room with a construction crew hard at work in his head. After restoring a little of his pride with the trick on Smythe, he'd left Relish's in search of another place where he could complete the buzz he'd started. He'd found Don Juan's, another popular watering hole, and closed the place.

It had been a tough couple of days. First, a stripper in a limo hoodwinked him, then he ran into Smythe – literally. The wine competition was just what he needed to take his mind off things.

A couple extra-strength Excedrin had helped with the hangover, and he'd killed time Sunday by visiting some wineries, getting some story ideas. He'd begun work on his laptop on the Central Coast story that included Kildeer. He finished it on Monday morning before he checked out, and e-mailed it to Samples, who had returned to Chicago on Sunday.

Will was still mad about that story. It really should have been the cover story. The problem was that Samples didn't have the palate to recognize a truly great wine like the Kildeer zin, and was more interested in the bottom line. But Samples was the boss, and Will wearily realized his argument was falling on increasingly deaf ears. Samples was determined to go with the Troublante story and its attendant advertising revenue, the better story be damned.

After lunch, he hit the road for Palm Springs. It would take him about eight hours, but he wanted to get there so he could play in the pre-competition golf tourney on Tuesday. It wasn't much of a tourney, really, just some of the golf-loving judges who got together for some fun, especially at the 19th hole. The hotel/resort had a conference center, spa and golf course all rolled into one, so the tourney participants teed off at noon Tuesday, and the judges' reception began at 6 that night, all at the same place. Beer flowed freely on the golf course, and by the third hole most of the golfing judges were having fun.

Will always wanted to be on the same team as Johnny Fine. Johnny was a Central Valley guy who had played on his college golf team before starting his winery in Sonoma County. His wines were always medal winners, adding to the luster of his brand, Fine Wines. Will loved the play on words. He also loved that nobody at the competition had Fine's golf game, and that by partnering with Johnny, they'd take the top prize, usually a gag gift that generated a lot of laughs at the Tuesday reception. Johnny always feigned surprise at winning, and sure enough, Will "won" a block of fake cheese because supposedly he ate more cheese as a palate cleanser during the competition's flights. It wasn't true, but who cared? Everyone howled.

Wednesday morning, Will was delighted to find he was on a marvelous panel. The Palm Springs competition organizers went to great lengths to have balanced panels; they wanted the perspectives of the various segments of the wine industry – winemakers, wine journalists, retailers and restaurateurs.

One of Will's favorite people on the judging circuit, Jill Corini, was on his panel. She was a slender Midwesterner who ran a wine shop in an Indianapolis suburb. Since Indy was only a couple hours from Chicago, he'd gone down there a few times for tastings at her shop. He'd even interviewed her for a Bung story he once did on the evolving Midwest wine scene. Neither was interested in a romantic entanglement, even though both were single, but they were great friends and always enjoyed one another's company. Their palates were in sync, which made for a fun judging panel, especially when the others were similarly attuned.

And this panel was that for sure. The winemaker, a large lass from Temecula, had a great palate, as did the restaurateur, a local guy from one of the desert cities' restaurants. It became clear on the first flight that theirs would be a special group. Organizers tried to spread the different categories around so that all the judges had some interesting wines, but they also had to endure some of the less thrilling varietals. The judges understood, looking forward to some of the more exciting varietals, such as zinfandel, syrah and sauvignon blanc, while being cheerful about sharing the heavy chardonnay load, a category that always had the largest number of entries since chardonnay was every winery's cash cow. The servers arrived with their first trays for Will's panel, with 12 chardonnays each, in wine glasses identified only by a number code. The panel's judges jotted down the numbers on their score sheets and went to work.

His story done, and Smythe forgotten for the moment, Will enjoyed the day, and was excited by some of the wines that they judged. Chardonnay had made way for pinot gris and gewürztraminer, followed by Rhone blends and sangiovese, an up and coming wine in California. He made some notes, jotting down some of the wines' number codes in anticipation of learning the identity of the wines at the end of the competition. A journalist always needed new grist for the mill. His panel wrapped up their first day by 3:30, giving Will a chance to check for messages before meeting Jill and the Temecula winemaker, Debbie (neither Will nor Jill could recall her last name, as they hadn't judged with her before), for a palate-cleansing beer before they headed for the judges' dinner.

Debbie excused herself a little after 4, pleading that she needed to check messages, leaving Will and Jill on the hotel veranda to finish their drinks. Will had been waiting for just such an opportunity because he wanted to get Jill's take on the Kildeer-Troublante stories.

After outlining the situation – major story getting buried to shill for the egotistical Troublante – Weinglas looked Jill in the eye and said, "I don't know what to do. We are going to look so stupid when the next issue comes out because everyone is talking about Kildeer. And we'll lead the mag with a puff piece. Dud is pissed because Smythe discovered this guy and we're playing catch-up, but Jill, I'm telling you: people read Smythe's stuff and look for us to fill in the details. Smythe doesn't have any details on Kildeer. Got any ideas on how I can make Dud see that?"

A foursome was teeing off at the resort's first hole, visible from where they were sitting, and Jill watched as the first guy took three or four practice swings, addressed the ball, and, swinging with all his might, topped the ball, sending it a whopping 75 yards, barely past the women's tee.

"Dud's motivation is money," she said, as the irked golfer reached down and snatched up his tee, while the second golfer began looking for a spot from which to launch his tee-shot. "He knows that Kildeer isn't going to spend a nickel on advertising, but that Troublante will spend thousands." They both glanced over as the second golfer unleashed a slice so pronounced that it landed in the adjacent fairway. Jill looked back at the intent Weinglas. "From an editorial perspective, you're right: the Kildeer story is much better. But from a business standpoint, I think Dud's right: Troublante will pay big bucks."

It was Will's turn to look at the golfers; the third guy let fly what would have been a prodigious blast, except that he had teed the ball too high, got under it, and sent it sky-high. It surpassed the first guy's shot – but not by much.

"I know that Troublante's loaded, but at what point have we sold our integrity, along with our space? Readers aren't stupid; they get it when we pander to the pompous."

The fourth golfer was waggling his driver, and somehow, with a smooth, even swing, managed to avoid the fate of his companions and hit a reasonable 200-yard drive right down the middle of the fairway. As Will and Jill watched, the first guy, sharing a cart with one of the other golfers, drove to where his anemic drive had come to rest, picked up the ball, and drove on out to the middle of the fairway a few yards short of the fourth man's drive, dropped his ball in the fairway, and prepared to hit his second shot.

"What a cheater!" murmured Jill. "Did you see that?"

Will was shaking his head, with a disbelieving smile.

"I think you have to look at both sides here," Jill said, returning to Will's dilemma. "I think the money won't hurt, but I think you can frame the Kildeer story around the fact that this is just breaking, you got it late, and you'll have more coming at a future date. That approach actually lets you do a more in-depth look at Kildeer and let your readers know what's really behind a hundred-point wine. I doubt you've had that time with this story."

Will had to admit his current story was rushed, but he still thought it a good effort, even though it was a bit diluted. He took a deep breath and exhaled. "You're probably right," he said. He had hoped Jill would side with him, but he knew the money was important to the magazine's continued health.

"I know what you're saying about Troublante," Jill continued. "She's kind of sleazy. I imagine she's pretty self-serving, whereas the Kildeers are probably down to earth. Am I right?"

Will nodded. "Yep, spot on."

"Even so, her opening is big news in Napa, plus the rest of the industry is watching. So it's not a bad cover story; there's interest there as well." She tipped her glass up, draining the last liquid. "Besides, not that many people subscribe to Smythe."

Will was looking at the bottom of his glass. "This is a strange industry," he said. "A couple years ago, I was in Sonoma County at a news conference with one of the industry's big-wigs. He was imploring the press to keep writing great stories and good reviews so the public would be interested and buy more wine. 'We need you,' he said. What other industry does that? Any other business, they'd buy an ad, but in the wine business you roll out the red carpet for a wine writer – take him to the best restaurants, put him up in the guest room at the winery – it's all hospitality. And after all that the writer doesn't dare say something bad about you. And essentially what you've bought is the integrity that comes with a news story."

"And I put up shelf-talkers and table-tents in my store to let them know that you loved the wine and so they should buy it," Jill said, smiling. "Or that it won a gold medal at this competition. Wine is still an intimidating beverage, and people feel more comfortable if someone tells them it's OK to buy it. Which is why you have a job. So cheer up! Let's get ready for the dinner."

Breakfast at Boobsie's was an event. Omelets were as much a trademark at Oak Pass's favorite eatery as burgers. Cork, Cathy and Bobby were all hard at work on three of Millie's signature creations – Italian sausage and spinach omelet for Cork; bacon and avocado for Cathy; chorizo and green chili for Bobby.

Tuesday had been another banner day for Kildeer Winery, and Cork and Cathy had stayed home, working in the tasting room, working on the winery's security, tending to chores that had been neglected since their lives had turned upside down. Cork called Bobby and arranged for the three of them to meet for breakfast Wednesday.

Over breakfast, they'd laid out their plan for Bobby. If Cathy had expected Bobby to try and talk them out of it, she would have been wrong. Cork knew Bobby: this was right in his friend's wheelhouse.

"Oh yeah, this could totally work," Bobby said. "I like it ... I *really* like this! Seriously, guys, it's a good plan."

"Why does it make me nervous when you say that?" Cork asked.

Bobby rolled his eyes. "OK, so whaddaya need from me?"

"Well, we need some IDs. She's a lawyer, so she'll want to see something that identifies us. Got any ideas?"

Bobby looked thoughtful for a few seconds, and then brightened. "Actually, yeah. You need badges."

"Badges?"

"Yep, gotcha covered. A friend o' mine works for the fire department and he owes me for getting this super hot chick..."

"Fire department badges?" Cathy asked, cutting off what she knew was about to be another "and that's how I lost my underwear" Bobby tale.

"Sure, just flash 'em quick and it'll look official enough. No worries."

They all stopped and looked at each other for a moment, the absurdity of what they were planning sinking in.

"Yep, no worries at all," Cork finally said, and they all burst out laughing.

Millie walked up with a coffee pot as the three were wiping their eyes, grinning at each other.

"What's up over here kids?"

"Funny you should ask, Millie," Cork said. He invited her to sit, then asked nonchalantly, "You ever do any acting, Millie?"

"Yeah, I dabbled in theater back in the day," she said. "Why do you ask?"

"Well, I've got a great supporting role in a stunt we're going to try and pull off." He filled her in on all that had happened that led to their crazy scheme.

"We need someone to call ahead, a supervising agent," Cathy said, making air quotes. "To make sure Troublante will be there. And we need someone who can sound tough."

"And a woman's voice, we think, would put Troublante off balance, a little," Cork added.

Boobsie's owner was quiet a moment, then stood and refilled their coffees. Cork and Cathy looked at each other, worried they'd asked too much of their friend.

"We're sorry," Cathy started. "We don't mean to put you on the spot...

"It's just that, well, we're scared, Millie, and, uh, a little desperate, in case you couldn't tell."

"Oh, stop!" Millie said, straightening, a huge grin spreading across her face. "I'm in! Can't wait to put the fear of God into that witch."

"Oh thank God!" Cathy said, grabbing the older woman's arm.

"Can you call her tomorrow afternoon, say, just before her winery closes?" Cork asked. The "agents" would be on her doorstep by midday Friday.

"Got it, no problem," Millie said. Then she pursed her lips. "I sure hope you can pull it off. It's risky, what you're trying."

"We have to," Cork said, determined.

"I knew you couldn't resist," Bobby said, winking at Millie, who smirked and headed back to the counter.

They looked at one another as an adrenalin rush hit them all as they realized what was about to happen.

"Cath, can you blend these stitches and my eyebrow together?"

"Yeah, I think so," she said. "I'll use an eyebrow pencil."

Bobby ticked off a list of tactics to employ: rent a small white car like feds usually drive; wear sunglasses, even inside, it makes people nervous; and, oh yeah, Bobby was going too.

"I dunno, Bobby. If anything goes wrong, you might not want to be involved."

"Hey, Cork, I'm already involved, remember? She thinks I'm you. But I wouldn't go in the winery. I was thinking more of parking outside her gate and cloggin' things up just in case you needed to make a hasty exit. Just in case…"

What the hell, thought Cork. "OK, sure why not? Reinforcements might not be such a bad idea."

"As if you could keep me out of this caper," Bobby said.

They raised their coffee mugs.

"To us," Bobby said.

"To Kildeer Ranch," Cathy added.

The judges' dinner Wednesday night was at a popular restaurant in Indian Wells, about a 40-minute drive from the competition hotel. The organizers provided a bus for the outing, but Will opted to take his rental car since he wanted to be able to return on his schedule, not the bus's. Jill and Debbie were happy to ride with him.

The dinner was at a place named Simple Pleasures, and it had a very simple menu: your choice of beef, chicken, fish or vegetarian. The fish changed virtually daily, but otherwise the menu was static.

Will ordered the beef steak offered that evening because he wanted to pair it with several of the red-wine medal winners available from previous years' competitions. Jill, a sparse eater, chose the salmon available that evening. Debbie, no stranger to the dinner table, also chose the steak. Asparagus was the vegetable du jour, although Debbie had the optional baked potato.

Simple Pleasures also happened to have a superb piano bar, and the judges enjoyed their post-dinner wine with the piano man, calling out song after song, or sending requests on cocktail napkins. The pianist was great, and played every request flawlessly. The wine judges made sure his tip jar was filled.

Jill only ate half her salmon and asked for it and her remaining asparagus in a to-go box while she enjoyed the piano tunes. Will had found a delightful pinot noir amidst the previous year's medal winners provided by the competition for the dinner, and sipped contentedly. Debbie turned out to be the life of the party, laughing and occasionally singing with the pianist. And darned if she didn't have a pretty good voice.

Those riding the bus left about 10 o'clock, leaving Will, Jill and Debbie, plus a couple others, to close out the pianist's last set. By 11:15 or so they were on their way back to Palm Springs. Rather than find his way out to the freeway, Will opted to follow the road back up through the desert cities to their hotel, thinking at that hour traffic would be light. Within a few minutes, he discovered the error of his ways: for some reason traffic was heavy, and they seemed to catch every light red.

Debbie was in the back seat, still singing, pretty well anesthetized from an evening of wine and song. Will wasn't paying much attention to her; she and Jill seemed to be having some sort of hazy conversation. He was focused on traffic and wondering why Jill always asked for a to-go box. When was she going to eat her leftovers? He knew that her habit would be to show up the next morning 5 minutes before the second day's judging was to begin, never bothering with breakfast. Perhaps she ate her leftovers for breakfast. But cold salmon and asparagus? He shuddered. Not his first choice.

What he thought would be a 30-to-40-minute ride was going to last more than an hour, he realized. And after 15 agonizing minutes, the traffic came to a stop. It would inch ahead, the stop again. Start, stop, start, stop.

Up ahead Will could see some bright lights on the road. Construction, he thought. Bummer. But as they crawled closer, he began to suspect that it wasn't a construction zone that was slowing traffic. There was no machinery, no workers. What the heck was going on?

Debbie was now giggling. And she had discovered Jill's leftover asparagus. She was taking the slender green spears and slurping them down like a child with spaghetti. She'd slurp one down and go, "Wheeeeee!!!"

Will lifted his foot off the brake pedal, and the car moved forward another few feet before he braked to a stop again. They were now about a hundred yards from the first bright light. As Will peered at the light, and the uniformed people milling about under it, it suddenly hit him.

"Sobriety checkpoint!" he yelled. "Quick, Chinese fire drill!" Jill reacted instantly, threw open her door simultaneously with Will, and they executed a perfect routine. As Will passed Jill at the rear of the car, he glanced at the traffic backed up behind him and saw that people had figured out why he was suddenly doing a Chinese fire drill and were starting to do the same; other cars were making U-turns and heading back the way they had come.

He jumped into the passenger seat, just as Jill slid into the driver's seat. Debbie was still working on the asparagus and going "Wheee!"

"What am I doing?!?" Jill blurted out. "I've been drinking, too!" Nonetheless she fastened her seatbelt and slid the gearshift from park to drive, and the car moved slowly forward. Will was speechless.

"Quick!" she said, "gimme that salmon!" Will turned in his seat and snatched the to-go box from Debbie, who appeared oblivious to what was happening, serenely smiling with closed eyes, and going "Wheeee!"

Jill grabbed some salmon from the open box with her bare hand and started cramming it in her mouth. She chewed that up, swallowed, and grabbed some more, flecks of salmon getting on her lips and cheeks. That went down, and she grabbed another mouthful, shoving it in.

By now they were within yards of the checkpoint, and Will could see that a woman sheriff's deputy was the first point of contact. The car in front of them was waved through, and they were next. Will held his breath. Jill let the car roll forward, still munching on salmon, and rolled down the window. The deputy held up her hand and Jill braked to a stop. The deputy leaned down toward Jill, then suddenly pulled back, a sour look on her face as the fish odor hit her. She quickly motioned Jill forward. Still chewing, Jill let the car roll forward, then gently pressed the gas pedal, and they moved off.

Neither of them said a word for the next few minutes, until Jill started to smile, and the smile turned into a chuckle, and then they were both laughing hysterically. Debbie snored blissfully in the back seat all the way back to the hotel.

ZINFORADO!

Chapter 11

THURSDAY, APRIL 21

J. Worthington Smythe couldn't have been more pleased with himself. This was the perfect plan. He'd laid it out for Josephine the day before, and she had become as excited as he was. It didn't matter that eventually Samples and Weinglas at the Bung would figure out who was behind the prank. In fact, he hoped they would.

"When should I place the call, Mr. Smythe?" she had asked. She always kept things formal.

"Early Thursday afternoon, say at 2," he said, knowing that would be 11 a.m. on the West Coast. "Then we watch as the fun starts." He chuckled. Piss on both of you, he thought, anticipating Samples' and Weinglas' reactions.

Josephine waited impatiently all morning, and Smythe was anxious for her to make the call as well. Finally, 2 o'clock arrived. Smythe was sitting in one of the two chairs across from Josephine's desk; he didn't want to miss a thing.

Josephine punched the speakerphone button, and a dial tone hummed at them. She dialed the area code and telephone number. On the second ring, a woman answered: "Good afternoon, Troublante Vineyards, how may I direct your call?"

"Laura Troublante, please," Josephine said.

"Who should I say is calling?" said Mindy Surlees, noticing the area code on her phone's caller ID window was 212.

"I'm a copy editor at The Wine Bung," Josephine said smoothly. "I'm editing a story for our next issue about Troublante Vineyards, and I just a had couple questions for her, if she's free."

"One moment," the woman's voice said, placing Josephine on hold.

Mindy punched a button on her phone, dialed an extension, and a moment later Laura Troublante picked up. "Yes?"

"A copy editor wants to speak with you about The Bung's cover story."

"OK, I'll get it in a minute." Troublante turned back to her computer screen.

Back in New York, Josephine was inspecting her fingernails as the silence continued – 30 seconds, 40, 50. "So far so good," Josephine said softly to J. Worthington. He nodded solemnly. A minute and a half went by, two minutes ... three. Finally, after three minutes and 27 seconds, Laura Troublante herself picked up the phone.

"Laura Troublante."

"Hello, Ms. Troublante," Josephine said quickly, "I'm a copy editor at The Wine Bung. I'm editing this story on Troublante Vineyards and just wanted to check a couple things with you."

"What's wrong this time?" Troublante said, irritation seeping into her voice. "I thought we got it all straightened out the last time you people called."

"Nothing wrong, I don't think," Josephine said smoothly. "I just wanted to double check some facts before we go to print. I hope you don't mind. This is such a big story, and we're thrilled to feature you on next month's cover. "

J. Worthington grinned, while 3,000 miles away Laura Troublante's irritation subsided at the flattery. She softened her tone. "Of course; what is it?"

"I just wanted to verify the year that you had intercourse with that judge in his chambers ..."

"What?!?" Troublante exploded. "What the hell does that have to do with the story? That was before I had a winery!"

Smythe's eyebrows shot up. So it's true, he thought, as Troublante continued her rant. He had once heard a rumor to that effect on one of his trips to California, but never gave it much credence. Until now. Wow, he thought.

"I didn't talk to Weinglas about that! What the hell is this? We have a deal! Who fed you that, anyway?"

"Ma'am, I'm just the copy editor trying to verify a fact. I don't know what arrangements you may have with Mr. Samples and Mr. Weinglas," Josephine calmly intoned. "Would you mind verifying the year?"

"I'll verify that your tits will get cut off if that gets in there," Troublante raged. "Where's Samples? Get him on the line!"

"Personal threats and insults are uncalled for, Ms. Troublante. Mr. Samples is out of the office, so if you'd like to speak with him, you'll have to call back. Now, about that date..."

"Aaarrrggghhhiiieeeekkkk!" and the phone slammed down.

Josephine turned to J. Worthington, whose face was already in a huge grin, and they started laughing.

At Troublante Vineyards, Laura rang Mindy's extension. "Get me Samples' number now!"

"Just a second ..." Mindy said, flipping through her Rolodex. "... It's 312..."

Dudley Samples was still out to lunch when Laura Troublante called his Chicago office at 1:17 p.m. Central time. The message she left on his voice mail might well have melted the phone had it been made of softer material. So when Samples returned to his office some 20 minutes later and retrieved the message, he was at once dumbfounded and petrified. What could possibly have set Laura off that way?

His hand visibly trembled as he dialed her direct line.

She picked up after the first ring. "Yes?" she asked curtly.

"Laura, it's Dudley…"

"You worthless pile of horse shit!" she snarled. "We had a deal! You're supposed to be writing about my winery, not my past career and other … other issues!"

"Laura, I assure you! I have no idea what you're talking about!" Samples was sweating slightly, and loosened his tie, suddenly aware that his starched collar felt tight around his neck.

"Your own copy editor just called me to check facts, and the first fact she's checking isn't about my winery, but about a court case before I even had a winery! I never told Weinglas about that. How'd that get in there? What the hell are you doing to me?"

"Nobody from this office called you today. The story's already been typeset. We're not checking any facts at this late date. The deadline for that's already passed. We don't have anything in there about past court cases. Laura, I assure you, whoever called you, it wasn't from here."

"You're not a very good liar, Samples."

"Laura, I have no reason to lie to you! I have nothing to gain and a whole lot to lose, so why would I?"

"I don't know, Samples, but I'll tell you what: you'd better get that lackey of yours, Weinglas, out here fast to answer some questions. 'Cause if you don't know anything about this, five'll get you 10 he does."

"Will's at a wine competition in Southern California; I'm sure he had nothing to do with this. I mean, how can you be so sure this wasn't some sort of prank?"

"Because it was too specific. The quote-unquote fact had to do with a specific case and my dealings with the judge. And your copy editor asked what was the date that I fucked the judge! Now who, besides you and Weinglas, would know that? That's not public knowledge."

Samples was stunned. He had no idea that Troublante had resorted to such tactics in her court dealings. I'm just a Midwestern magazine publisher, he thought. How the hell would I know anything about some California court case? Could Will have possibly known about something like that? He was from California, after all, so perhaps he'd heard something on the grapevine.

"Laura, I can assure you ..."

"You already said that!"

"Well I'll say it again! I assure you that there is nothing in our cover story on you and your winery that even suggests you've ever had sexual relations with a judge, or anyone else for that matter. And furthermore, I had no idea you had sex with a judge. But I'll call Will and tell him to come see you and reassure you."

"He'd better have a copy of the story with him so I can ascertain if you're telling the truth."

"Ethically I can't let you read a story in advance of publication. That constitutes censorship."

"You pathetic hypocrite. The only reason you're doing this story is because I'm spending thousands of dollars on advertising. So get over your fucking ethics, and get Weinglas up here with a copy of that story!"

The slamming phone reverberated in Samples' ear. Slowly he put down the phone and leaned back in his chair. He shook his head. What a mess! Only one thing to do, he thought: get Will up there and straighten this whole thing out.

It was a couple minutes after noon on the West Coast, and Will and the rest of his panel were just wrapping up their last flight of wines before breaking for lunch when a hotel staffer brought Will a pink message slip. It read: Please call Dudley Samples, and his office number. Dud could wait a couple minutes, he thought.

His panel finished doling out the medals on the flight. It had been a particularly exciting flight of syrahs with three gold medals awarded so far out of the 12 wines in the flight, and there were a couple wines yet to go. Will had scored one of those last two wines a gold on his score sheet, and he wanted to see what it would end up with.

Seven minutes later, the panel headed for lunch. Will found a house phone and returned Samples' call, a smile spreading from ear to ear. The last wine, the one he had scored a gold, had been a unanimous choice of the panel for gold, and as a result was headed for the sweepstakes round where it would be considered by all the judges, working as a panel of the whole, for best red wine of the competition, and possibly best overall wine of the competition. The panel had concluded its morning work on a high note.

The phone rang in his ear, and he heard the familiar words: "Dudley Samples."

"Hi Dud, you just called. What's up?"

"I just had a call from a raving Laura Troublante, who said one of our copy editors just called to verify the date of when she had sex with a judge. Said it was in your story. Do you know anything about that?"

"I have no clue what you're talking about," Will said, totally perplexed.

"I read your story, and I don't recall anything like that. Did you add anything after I'd seen it?"

"No, I didn't touch it after I turned it in."

"Did you know that Troublante once screwed a judge who was presiding over a case she was involved with?"

"What? No! I never heard anything like that."

"C'mon, Will, you're from California. You didn't hear any rumors about that?"

"Dud, I'm telling you, I don't know anything about that. I didn't know Laura Troublante until we started working on this story about her. You said a copy editor asked her about it?"

"That's what she said. I've asked our copy editors and nobody here called her. So I'm trying to figure out what the hell this is all about. You're sure you don't know anything?"

"Dud, I swear to you, I have no idea where this would have come from."

"OK, OK, but you've got to get up there and reassure her that there's nothing in the story about that. Show her the story if you have to. You got a copy with you?"

"Yeah, but that's not kosher."

"I don't give a damn whether it is or not!" snapped Samples. "You get up there by tomorrow at the latest and convince her that we're not reporting on anything but her winery. I don't know where she got this idea, or who called her, but we've got to put a stop to it as soon as possible."

"Tomorrow? Dud, the competition should wrap up before noon ..."

"Will, fuck the competition! This is our livelihood we're talking about here! Drive, fly – I don't care. Just get up there and convince her that we're above board."

Will's heart sank a little. He didn't want to confront an angry Laura Troublante. But he realized he had no choice. His shoulders sagged. "OK, Dud, I'll leave first thing in the morning," he said in a resigned voice. "It's an eight or nine hour drive up there from here, or maybe I can find a flight."

"Thanks, Will. Call me as soon as you meet with her."

"OK, no problem. Talk to you tomorrow." He hung up.

"Problems?" The voice was behind him. He turned to see Jill who had been waiting for him to go to lunch.

He sighed. "Yes, I'm sorry to say. I'll have to miss the sweepstakes round; Dud wants me to head up to Napa tomorrow to meet with Laura Troublante over some misunderstanding about the story I did on her. I'll have to leave in the morning. It's 500 miles up there, so I hope I can catch a flight."

"Bummer. But you're good for this afternoon? Still going to be at the dinner tonight?"

"Yeah, there's no point in leaving this afternoon; if I drove, it'd probably be midnight by the time I got there, and I probably wouldn't get to see her until late in the morning anyway. So I'll just leave early."

"Well, then, let's get something to eat before we have to go back to work. You can worry about Laura Troublante later. We've got chicken-Caesars for lunch."

About 3 o'clock, the phone rang at Troublante's, and was answered by Mindy: "Troublante Vineyards, how may I direct your call?"

"Good afternoon, this is Jane Deer from the BATF." Millie Bounty was speaking in her most authoritative tone from her office in Boobsie's. Cork and Cathy were sitting nearby.

"Yes? How may I help you?" Mindy said, affecting a formal tone.

"I'd like to speak to Laura Troublante. Is she available?"

Mindy swallowed. "Uh, she has someone in her office right now," recalling how her boss had summoned Damien and given instructions not to be disturbed. Mindy knew what was happening in there. She also was aware of the calls between Troublante and the copy editor and Samples, and knew that when Troublante became stressed, she needed relief. Damien's special talents helped restore her equilibrium. "May I take a message, or may I help you?"

"We have a report of unauthorized port production at this facility," Millie intoned. "We'll have two agents at your facility about 11 o'clock tomorrow morning to investigate this report, agents Fisher and Henry. I'm calling to ensure that Ms. Troublante will be there to meet with the agents and answer their questions."

Mindy's blood ran cold. Oh my God! She thought. How did they find out about that? What are we going to do?

"Miss, are you there?"

"Uh, yes. Yes, I'll inform Ms. Troublante."

"Do you have any questions?"

"No, no questions."

"All right then, tomorrow morning, 11 o'clock, agents Fisher and Henry. Got that?"

"Yes, 11 o'clock. I'll let Ms. Troublante know."

Millie hung up. She looked at Cork and Cathy. Cathy had a sly smile.

"Where'd you come up with those names?" she asked.

Millie shrugged. "My first husband's last name was Fisher – I always called him that – and my second husband was named Henry. So they were just sorta the first names that popped into my head."

"OK, then," Cork said. "I'll be Fisher, you're Henry." They all chuckled.

"You got your car rented?" Millie asked.

"Yep, we're picking it up as soon as we leave here," Cork said.

"Bobby get you the badges?"

"Yep, got those, too."

"OK, kids, the die is cast," Millie said. She smiled then winked at the young couple. "Be safe tomorrow."

Some 250 miles to the north, Mindy was looking at the phone she had just hung up, and started to panic. She had never understood why Troublante had bothered with the phony port in the first place. She had slowly come to the conclusion that the "port" was Troublante's way of flipping off the wine establishment. If she wasn't quite desperate to be accepted by the vintners, she was certainly determined. But the wine community was noticeably cool toward her. She felt her wealth gave her entry. More accurately she was looking to be embraced. And when she wasn't, resentment began to build.

The funny thing was the stuff actually tasted pretty good – sweet and a bit nutty. Mindy liked it, but knew full well it was illegal as hell. She wondered if telling

Cork Kildeer had been such a good idea. Surely he wouldn't have told anyone about it. He was such a charmer.

Damn it! That stuff is going to get us in trouble! It had been 45 minutes since Troublante had closeted herself with Damien, but Mindy decided this couldn't wait. She strode to Troublante's private office and knocked loudly on the door.

To her surprise, Troublante said, "Come in." When Mindy entered, she found Troublante reclining on the couch in her office, gazing out the window and holding a glass of white wine, clad in a bathrobe open down the front. How pastoral, Mindy thought, mindful that the relaxed Troublante was about to become the enraged Troublante.

"I'm sorry to bother you, but I just got a call from the BATF. They're coming tomorrow to talk to you about the port."

Troublante's languid gaze suddenly flashed fire. "What? What do you mean?"

"A woman agent said they'd heard reports of, how'd she say it?" She paused: "'Unauthorized port production' here. They're coming to investigate. She asked if you'd be here at 11 tomorrow morning to answer questions."

What next? Troublante thought. First the Bung, now this. Those nincompoops at the Bung were one thing, but this was something else. The feds were not to be trifled with. Still, her tryst with Damien had left her mind crystal clear. First, she decided, we'll hide the stuff. And the agents will no doubt be a couple of pencil pushers who will turn to putty in my hands. Men are so easy to manipulate.

Mindy stood there expecting to be flogged as the bearer of bad news. But instead Troublante said, "OK, we're going to move it, hide it somewhere. How many cases do we have?"

"Of the port? Oh, 400 or so."

"Do you have a garage at your place?"

Mindy didn't like where this was going, but said, "Yes, but I put my car in it."

"Well, park it in the driveway for the next couple days!" Troublante snapped. "We're going to hide it in your garage until the feds leave. We'll move it back here as soon as we get rid of them. How far away is your place?"

Mindy suddenly felt trapped. She was being forced to be directly involved with an illegal scheme, and she wasn't at all comfortable about it. She lived about eight miles south of the winery, in Napa, she told Troublante in a quiet voice.

"Perfect!" Troublante exclaimed. "I'll get a couple of guys from shipping-and-receiving to load it up and take it over there."

Mindy was starting to wish she'd never met Laura Troublante.

Cork and Cathy had left Millie's excited and nervous at the same time. Their plan was now launched. They had seized the initiative and were moving forward. They drove the few miles to Bobby's place to let him know the plan was in motion.

The Clover was packed, as usual, and Cork and Cathy had to squeeze past patrons to find Bobby pouring large "tastes" at the bar he and Cork had made out of some oak beams Bobby said he'd found at a tumbled down shed.

"We'll leave at 6 in the morning, and should get to Troublante's about 11," Cork said.

"Roger that," Bobby grinned. This was turning into a grand adventure for him. He finished ringing up a customer, then let his employee, Sharon, know he'd be out a few minutes. He walked Cork and Cathy to the parking lot.

"I'll be at your place by 6. Now, what I plan to do when we get there is just park out on the shoulder in front of the winery. I'll stay in the truck, so don't worry about them seeing me. As soon as you leave, I'll wait there a few minutes to make sure everything's OK, then follow you. When we get to San Jose, let's rendezvous at Original Joe's and have lunch and figure out what we got."

With their schedule set, Cork and Cathy headed home, arriving about 5:30. The tasting room was just closing after another banner day. They helped the tasting room workers close up, bid them good evening, and double-checked that all was secure. They strolled over to their house, and plopped down in chairs at the kitchen table.

Neither felt like cooking, but they didn't feel like going out either, so they ordered pizza. The guy who took their order told them it would be 45 minutes to an hour before their pizza got there.

So they opened a bottle of zinfandel and poured themselves each a glass. Cork lifted his glass, and looked into Cathy's eyes.

"Here's hoping we can pull this off," he said. Cathy slowly smiled, and clinked his glass with hers.

"Here's to us," she said softly.

Chapter 12

FRIDAY, APRIL 22

It was still dark at 4:30 in the morning, but it may as well have been high noon as far as Cork and Cathy were concerned. They both were wide awake and jittery with anticipation. They abandoned any pretense of sleeping. Cathy showered while Cork brushed his teeth; they traded places without turning off the shower. A few minutes later they were figuring out what to wear.

Some 250 miles north, Mindy was already exhausted. She'd been up all night while Damien and a guy from shipping-and-receiving stacked some 400 cases of Troublante Vineyards' "port" in her garage. All that was left of the stuff at the winery was a few stray bottles in the lab, and she was too tired to care about them. She had become increasingly bitter about the role she was being forced to play. It was one thing to go the extra mile for your boss; it was something else again to be asked – hell, told! – to do something illegal. She made a mental note to start looking for another job come Monday. Maybe teaching wasn't such a bad choice after all.

And some 250 miles south of Oak Pass, Will was hanging up his wake-up call and getting ready to hop in the shower before checking out and heading for the airport to catch the morning flight to Sacramento. He'd been able to book a seat on the 7 a.m. flight that would take him first to LAX, and then after changing planes, on to SMF, arriving about 10 a.m. He'd also reserved a rental car from the same company as the one he was driving. He figured that on a Friday morning the traffic shouldn't be too bad, and that he'd be able to make the drive from Sacramento International Airport to Troublante Vineyards before noon. With any luck at all, he thought, he'd be able to catch the 11:31 redeye that night out of SFO for O'Hare; he'd reserved a seat at the same time he booked his flight to Sacramento.

Cork and Cathy knew that to pull this stunt off, they'd need to look the part. They knew that federal field agents didn't dress too formally, but neither did they dress too casually. Their appearance needed to be somewhere in between, something that, at first glance, left no doubt that they meant business.

They decided to both wear black pants. Cathy also opted for black flats, a white V-neck blouse and a royal blue jacket. To accentuate her cleavage she wore a demi-bra. She was keenly aware that women checked one another's figures, and for power players like Laura Troublante bust size mattered. Someone like Troublante was worse than a man in that regard: she sized up her opponent, and calculated her strategy based on the woman's figure.

Cathy's demi would accentuate her own large breasts, and the V-neck blouse would reveal enough to send Troublante a subtle message that I'm not susceptible to your tricks.

Cork put on a pale blue shirt with button-down collar, sans tie. The BATF agents he'd seen locally hadn't worn ties, except on one occasion when the agent was from Los Angeles. He pulled a medium-gray sport coat from the closet to complete his ensemble.

They looked at each other, smiled. "I think we might just pull this off," Cork said softly.

"You don't think this looks too racy do you?" Cathy asked, suddenly seized by a pang of self-consciousness, aware of her visible cleavage.

"No, I think you look perfect."

She cocked her head, twitched her mouth and raised an eyebrow.

"Really!" he said.

She broke into a big smile. "OK," she said. "A couple of government agents for sure."

Cork looked at his watch: "5:37," he said. "Bobby should be here in a few minutes. Let's have a quick bowl of cereal."

They went into the kitchen where Cork fixed two bowls of corn flakes. Wordlessly they munched the corn flakes; when they were finished, Cork rinsed the bowls and spoons and put them in the dishwasher.

Then they headed out to the rental car, turning out the house lights and locking the door behind them.

The early morning sky was getting lighter as Bobby pulled into their driveway. He lowered the driver's-side window.

"Ready, guys?" Bobby grinned.

"Let's do it," Cork replied.

Cork and Cathy climbed into their rental, and followed Bobby to the freeway ramp north. At that hour of the morning, with little traffic, they were at freeway speed almost instantly.

Cathy enjoyed the countryside as they passed a couple villages, vineyard land and rangeland dotted with California oaks. She was conscious that her husband was troubled. Normally he would have been talkative, but he was clearly deep in thought. About 45 minutes passed before she finally said, "Penny for your thoughts."

Cork didn't answer right away. His wife had been right: he had been pondering their predicament. After a couple minutes, he finally said, "Cath, It's hard for me to believe this is happening to us. One of the reasons I wanted to have our own brand was as a testament to Dad and Grandpa's hard work and commitment to growing good grapes and being good stewards of the land. I wanted it to be something you and I could share, something we could be proud of, something that at the end of the day we could share a glass of our wine and know we had given it our best. I sure hope it's been worth it."

He glanced at his wife. She had a slight smile. "It has for me," she said.

Cork focused on the road ahead for a few minutes. Then he said, "It's hard for me to understand someone like Laura Troublante. It seems to me that we celebrate our neighbors' successes. I mean if Bobby or Travis, or any of the others, got a hundred for one of their wines I'd be thrilled for them. But I wouldn't try to hijack their success, ya know what I mean?"

He glanced again at Cathy. She was looking at him intensely. "Yeah," she said softly, "I sure do." Then she added: "Don't worry, babe, we won't fail."

They reached simultaneously for each other's hand, and squeezed.

Their drive north continued without incident. The Friday morning rush hour had pretty well thinned out by the time they got to San Jose. They took the east side freeway, going up the East Bay, over the Benicia Bridge to the cutoff over to Napa. After four hours on the road, Cork was ready for a stretch, and detoured to a Starbucks in a shopping center at the freeway intersection. The three of them each ordered a Grande house blend – Bobby also had a piece of coffee cake – and sat at a vacant table near the front door. It was 10:05 a.m.

After each took a sip of the piping hot coffee, Cork said, "OK, we ready? We should be there right about 11. Let's hope it goes smoothly."

"Amen, brother," Bobby said.

"Just remember what TR told us about how these agents operate," Cork said. Cathy and Bobby both nodded.

He looked at his wife. "Are you OK with taking the lead on this?"

Cathy nodded. "Yeah, don't worry, babe."

Cork was still a little uneasy about the strategy. He was used to making decisions but now he was just a supporting actor without any lines. But he recognized this strategy offered them the best chance of success.

"You got it," he said, nodding to his wife. He noticed the cold resolve in her eyes. Laura Troublante doesn't stand a chance, he thought.

They headed for their respective cars, putting on their sunglasses as they walked. They got into their vehicles, backed out, exited the parking lot, and headed for the onramp, Cork and Cathy in the lead. As they were pulling back onto the freeway, none of them noticed the silver rental car pulling into Starbuck's.

Will Weinglas was ready for some coffee after navigating three airports, landing on time at Sacramento International, and getting to the freeway bypass toward San Francisco. He spotted a Starbucks and moved into the right lane. He didn't notice the little white car and pickup that were heading up the freeway on-ramp as he was exiting.

He parked, entered the Starbuck's, and asked for Venti Caffé Mocha. As he sat and sipped his drink, he still wondered what the hell he was doing there, and what had set Laura Troublante off. Shit, he thought, this is a puff piece, not an exposé. Oh well, we'll see what it's all about soon enough.

He decided to check in with Samples. At the gas station next to the Starbucks he found a pay phone. He dropped in some coins and dialed. "Hi Dud," he said when Samples came on the line. "I landed in Sacramento a little while ago. Just stopped for coffee. I'm heading to Troublante's right now. Should be there inside an hour."

"OK, good. See if you can figure out what the hell happened."

Will assured him he would, and concluded the call. His drink had cooled enough that he could take bigger swigs. Two minutes later, he finished his Mocha and headed for his car.

Cork, Cathy and Bobby made it through the last stoplight on the north end of Napa, and in less than two minutes were approaching the palatial Troublante Vineyards. Cork raised an eyebrow at the grandiosity of the place. As a college student, he'd visited Napa Valley many times and was well familiar with some of the large wine estates on either side of the highway as one drove north through the valley. Those places had history, but this was way over the top, he thought. The garish opulence of a French chateau plopped right in the middle of America's most famous wine region seemed out of place. No wonder tongues were clicking, he thought.

Cork flipped on the turn signal, and turned underneath the ornate archway into the driveway. Bobby kept going about 500 feet, pulled over at a wide spot, then, when traffic cleared for a moment, made a U-turn, and parked in front of the wall that bordered the Troublante property, just before the gate. The wall was about three-feet high along most of the frontage, allowing passersby to see the estate. It began a gradual slope upwards about 40 feet from the gate to a height of eight feet at the pillars that held the archway. His truck couldn't be seen from the chateau.

While the wall hid his truck, it also prevented him from seeing anything. So he pulled as close to the entrance as possible, switched off the motor, climbed out, walked around to the front of the truck and crouched down, hoping that passersby would think he was checking his tires. From this vantage point, he could peer through the gate and see when Cork and Cathy left.

Cork parked in the huge parking lot – it had space for about 100 cars, he guessed – switched off the engine, and glanced at Cathy. He breathed in deeply, and slowly exhaled. She gave him a tight grin as if to say here we go, and they got out of the car. Pulling on their jackets, they paused for a moment and looked at one another. "Think we pass muster?" Cork said.

"I believe so, Agent Fisher," Cathy grinned.

They laughed, which helped alleviate their tension. "OK, Agent Henry, here we go."

The two of them headed up the stamped-concrete walkway past the fountain and exquisite courtyard landscaping, toward the entrance. The sidewalk lead to a large mahogany doorway, the same one Bobby had entered earlier that month. They went in and, like

Bobby, gaped at the larger-than-life portrait of Laura Troublante.

"My God," Cork said.

"Yeah, narcissistic much? I mean ... wow."

Cork nudged his wife and pointed to a set of double French doors through which they could see the receptionist's desk. They opened the right door and went in.

An attractive young woman, her blonde hair in a short bob, was studying the computer screen on her desk. Mindy looked up when Cork and Cathy entered. It was 11:04.

"Hello. May I help you?" she said.

"Yes," Cathy said, "Agents Henry and Fisher, BATF." She reached into her purse, pulled out the fireman's leather-clad badge and flashed it momentarily under Mindy's nose before snapping it shut. Mindy's eyes widened for a moment as she glimpsed the shiny metal. "I believe you received a call from our office yesterday advising you that we'd be here. We'd like to speak with Laura Troublante."

Mindy was momentarily taken aback. It hadn't occurred to her that one of the agents would be a woman. But she quickly regained her composure. "Ah, yes, uh, just a moment, let me see if I can find her for you."

"I would hope so," Cathy said coldly. "It was made clear what time we would be here and that we wanted to speak with her."

"Uh, yes, a poor choice of words, sorry. I'll go find her." Mindy quickly exited through an unmarked door at the back of the room.

Cathy glanced at Cork. "So far so good," she said under her breath.

"Keep your fingers crossed," he said softly in reply.

A slightly undone Mindy walked down the hall to Laura Troublante's office, knocked, and entered when Laura said, "Come in."

"The agents are here," she told Troublante.

"I'll be out in a few minutes," Troublante replied. "Let them cool their heels for awhile."

Mindy noticed that her boss was dressed for the part, wearing a scoop-neck dress that extended past where her bra would have been had she been wearing one. It occurred to her that her boss had assumed that the agents would be two men, just as she, Mindy, had.

"I'm not sure that's such a good idea," Mindy said anxiously. "They appear to mean business."

"All the more reason to let them stew a bit," Laura said. It was a tactic she had learned as a lawyer. Making people wait tended to make them more nervous and malleable. She waved her hand at Mindy, shooing her out.

Mindy returned to the reception area two minutes after she had left. "Ms. Troublante will be with you shortly," she said with a forced smile. "Won't you have a seat?" She motioned to some chairs in the waiting area.

Cathy looked at Cork, then back at Mindy. Something boiled up inside her. This Troublante woman had sent someone to ruin their business, someone who had tried to cripple her husband, or worse, and sued them... Cathy's anger was real.

"Perhaps I didn't make myself clear," she said. "We have an appointment, so if Ms. Troublante can't seem to find her way out here, we'll find her." With that Cathy walked past the desk – Cork quickly caught his cue and followed – and before a startled Mindy could say anything, was through the door and down the hallway toward Troublante's office.

She didn't bother to knock.

Troublante looked up when Cathy and Cork – Agents Henry and Fisher – walked in, Mindy trailing behind them. They stared at one another for a couple seconds. Cathy and Cork had the same thought: so this is the person who's trying to ruin us.

"What's the meaning of this?" Troublante asked sharply.

"The meaning is that we're Agents Henry and Fisher of the BATF, and we have an appointment with you," Cathy said in as sharp a tone as Troublante's. She flashed the fireman's badge quickly past Troublante's face before snapping the leather case shut. "We are not some cork salesmen or distributor's representatives who you can leave twiddling their thumbs in your reception area. We're agents of the federal government.

"And we're here," Cathy continued icily, "to investigate reports of unauthorized port production at this facility. We'll start by looking at your fortification records."

Her hands bunched into fists, Cathy leaned forward on the desk on both sets of knuckles, allowing Troublante to quickly ascertain that Cathy was as well-endowed as she was.

Laura Troublante was stunned. This woman was the lead BATF agent? And she had stormed right into her office? Troublante realized that her "breast offensive" would have no effect on this agent. She opened her mouth, but no words formed as she stared at the angry "Agent Henry." Mindy didn't know what to think; she'd never seen her boss speechless.

Cathy's adrenalin was giving her a rush, and she realized that she couldn't back off now. She squeezed her eyes into narrow slits and leaned farther forward, mere inches from Troublante's face. "Was I somehow not clear?"

Troublante recovered somewhat from her initial surprise. She now tried to gain the initiative. "I'm afraid there's been some mistake," she said smoothly. "We don't have any port here."

"No?" said Cathy. "Then why would we have received a report that you do?"

"Well, we have this port-style wine ..."

Cathy cut her off. "Semantics! Port, port-style wine – we don't give a damn what you call it! Where are your fortification records?"

"We, uh ... that is, perhaps you'd like to see the facility and you'll see we don't make any port..."

Troublante had started to get up from her desk but Cathy cut her off.

"You're stalling, Ms. Troublante! We want to see your fortification records, and WE WANT TO SEE THEM NOW!" she yelled, slamming her hand flat on the desktop.

Troublante literally jumped at the sound. "We, uh, don't have any immediately available," she finally said.

Cathy looked at Cork, scrunching up the right side of her mouth and shaking her head. "Can you believe that, Agent Fisher?" she said, as Cork slowly shook his head as well. "Making a fortified wine and not keeping any fortification records."

Cork couldn't resist: "I'm amazed, Agent Henry," he deadpanned. "Tsk, tsk."

Cathy turned back to Troublante. "What the hell are you doing? Using brandy you bought at the supermarket?"

Laura Troublante blanched; Mindy's eyes bulged. How in the hell did she come up with that?

"Since you don't have any records," Cathy said, "we'll need to take a sample for analysis."

Cathy and Cork both recognized the look of panic that swept Troublante's face. But she quickly covered it up. "That won't be possible unless I see some paperwork authorizing you to take my personal property." The lawyer in her had reasserted itself.

"Agent Henry" didn't miss a beat. Remembering the story that Travis had told, she said in a voice dripping with condescension, "You want authorization, do you? Well let me put it to you this way, Mizzz Troublante, either you come up with a sample in the next 10 seconds of – let's see, what did you call it? Oh yeah – your 'port-style wine,' or we'll slap a chain and padlock on your front door so fast it'll make your head spin.

"If I recall from your bond application you're a lawyer by training. But Agent Fisher and I don't really care who or what you are. You can spend as much time and resources – uh, that's money, Mizzz Troublante – trying to get that padlock removed, but it won't go anywhere until we're satisfied that you're in compliance with the law and the terms of your bond. Now what's it going to be?"

Troublante felt like she'd just been flattened by a semi. If she refused to give them the sample, she'd have the shame and embarrassment of having the BATF shut her down. That sure wouldn't play well with Napa cognoscenti. She had no choice.

"Mindy," she said resignedly, "go get the agents a bottle of the port-style wine," her voice smoldering with hatred. Nobody had ever beaten her down like that, especially not in her own office in front of a staff member.

"Right away, Ms. Troublante." Mindy was only too anxious to disappear.

"Now that's much more reasonable," Cathy said in an exaggerated tone. She turned toward Cork. "You see, Agent Fisher? She can be reasonable." Cathy knew she was rubbing salt in the wound, but couldn't resist.

Troublante glared at her. She just glared back.

Two minutes and 49 seconds later Mindy returned, and handed Cathy a bottle of the wine that said only "Zinfandel," and 16.5 percent alcohol. Cathy looked at it, and handed it to Cork. He looked at it and nodded.

"Thank you, Ms. Troublante, that will be all today," Cathy said. "We'll be in touch."

She and Cork exited the office, headed back down the hallway, through the reception area, into the foyer past that gawd-awful portrait, out the front door and around the sidewalk leading to where they'd parked. Then they saw him.

Will Weinglas seemed to catch every red light through Napa. Also, a wide-load semi hauling two stainless steel fermentation tanks to some winery had difficulty making a turn, causing him to sit through one light twice. Once past, he proceeded at normal speed to Troublante Vineyards.

As he approached the entrance, he noticed a pickup on the shoulder behind the wall with a man crouched by the front tire. Car trouble, he mused, though he thought it a bit odd that the man was looking in the gate rather than attempting to identify the pickup's problem. No matter.

He turned on his left blinker and turned into the winery's entrance. The tasting room had only been open since 11, and few cars were in the massive parking lot. Mentally he winced, remembering what had happened a few days ago at this very place.

He parked his rental near a small white car and began walking toward the entrance. Just as he was nearing the mahogany doors, a man and a woman came out.

As they turned toward him, he suddenly recognized them. "Hi Cork, hi Cathy," he said pleasantly, pushing up his glasses. "You're the last people I expected to see here. What's going on?"

As soon as they saw Weinglas, the Kildeers almost started running. "Steady," Cork said under his breath. There was nothing to do but brazen it out.

"Oh, not much," Cork said. "Sorry we can't stay and visit, but we're on a kind of tight schedule. Hope you can come see us at the winery again soon." They kept walking.

"I'll take you up on that," Will said. "Say, is Laura in the office today?"

"She sure is," Cork tried to sound as lighthearted as possible. But he was suddenly wound tight as a drum. "See ya."

That was kind of abrupt, Weinglas thought, but kept walking to the front door and opened it, turned right through the foyer and into the business offices. Nobody was in the receptionist's area, but he could hear Laura Troublante's agitated voice down the hallway. Oh great, he thought, what has Dud got me into?

He walked down the hall to find Troublante verbally blasting Mindy, who was arguing back. He didn't know what to make of the situation, but obviously something was amiss. He hoped it wasn't his story they were discussing.

"... nothing to do with it!" Mindy was yelling as Will walked in. Both women suddenly turned and stared at him.

"Hi Laura, how's it going?" Will said hopefully.

"Oh, just peachy," she replied sarcastically. "You bring a copy of that story?"

"Yeah, but I'm still not sure what the problem is. By the way, what were the Kildeers doing here?"

"The who?"

"Cork and Cathy Kildeer, you know, from Kildeer Ranch down in Oak Pass? I just saw them leaving your office."

"What? No, those were uh..." she stopped herself before saying they were BATF agents. "No. I met Cork Kildeer here at the reception a week ago. That wasn't him."

"I'm telling you, that was Cork and Cathy Kildeer. I know them. I've interviewed them."

"No, those were ..." Her voice drifted off as the situation suddenly hit Troublante. She put her hand to her lips and whispered, "Oh no!" It was so soft that Weinglas barely heard her. She stared at Weinglas for three seconds, then suddenly yelled, "Damien!!!" and rushed toward the door.

She almost ran into Damien as he was coming in. "Those two agents who were just here? Stop them! They're not agents!"

Damien didn't ask questions, but turned and ran down the hallway toward the front door, with Laura right behind him. Will was bewildered: what the hell just happened?

Bobby Vangree recognized Weinglas as he turned into Troublante Vineyards' driveway, and went on full alert. He watched as Weinglas parked and started walking toward the entry. Then Cork and Cathy came out the front door. He watched as they interacted briefly with Will, then continued to their car.

Bobby figured that Weinglas would blow their cover within minutes of meeting with Troublante, so he hustled back to his pickup and got in. He started the engine, and lowered the windows so he could hear what was happening. He heard a car approaching the entry; it was Cork and Cathy. They stopped opposite him, and Cork gave him the thumbs-up sign.

"Great," Bobby yelled, "but that looked like Will Weinglas who you guys ran into."

"It was."

"Then get outa here, 'cause I betcha all hell's about to break loose. I'll meet you at the rendezvous."

It was getting close to noon, and traffic on the main Napa Valley highway was heavier than it had been earlier. Cork had to wait several seconds before he was able to turn onto the roadway heading south. Just as he did, Bobby heard a scream from Laura Troublante: "There they are! Stop them!"

Bobby heard a car door slam and an engine start. Then he heard tires screeching as the car – in fact it was the nine-passenger SUV that Damien had used to transfer the "port" to Mindy's garage – barreled toward the entry. He gauged when the SUV would reach the entry, and quickly accelerated, pulling his pickup directly across the entry.

Damien couldn't believe his eyes when a pickup suddenly lurched in front of him. He slammed on the brakes and turned to the left, but it was too late. The SUV struck the bed of the pickup just behind the rear tire, spinning it 180 degrees.

The impact also caused Damien to veer farther left, and the front of the SUV slammed into the edge of the wall behind which Bobby had been hiding. A telltale wisp of steam that grew by the moment indicated that Damien wasn't going very far, at least in that vehicle.

Bobby was momentarily dazed as a result of his sudden 180-degree spin, but quickly regained his senses. He jumped out of his pickup to ascertain the damage. The side panel behind the wheel-well was crunched in, but the wheel had sustained no damage; he could drive. He looked over at the big SUV and saw Damien staring at him. Recognition dawned on Damien's face – he had seen this man before – but still thought the face he was looking at belonged to Cork. Funny, he thought, he isn't dressed like an agent; I wonder what Laura was thinking?

A slow smile crept onto Bobby's face; he waved at Damien, turned and jumped back in his pickup, flipped a U-turn and headed south down the highway. He was unaware of a slow seep of brake fluid accumulating at a section of the brake line that had been pinched but not severed in the crash. His cursory check had not detected it.

Damien opened his door and got out, just as Laura came running up to him. His arms and shoulders, which had absorbed the impact of the crash, were sore.

"Goddammit, Damien, you've got to stop them!" Troublante screamed at him. She didn't hear the distant wail of a patrol car's siren; a passerby had called 911.

But Damien did. "I think we'll have to wait until the cops are done," he intoned. His head was starting to hurt. "Who were those guys anyway?"

"That was Cork and Cathy Kildeer! They were posing as BATF agents, and I gave them a bottle of the port!"

"Really? Well I just saw Cork Kildeer driving a pickup; he pulled in front of me and caused this wreck. It was the same guy who came to our reception a week ago. Where'd you get the idea that those other two were the Kildeers?"

"Weinglas told me! He's interviewed them and knows them. I have no idea who the other guy is."

"Lemme see if I got this straight," Damien said, closing his eyes and rubbing his forehead with his thumb and forefinger. "You're saying that the guy I just ran into, who came here a week ago who we thought was Cork Kildeer isn't Cork Kildeer, and the real Cork Kildeer and his wife were just here posing as BATF agents? And you just handed them a bottle of the stuff I spent all night hauling out of here to hide?"

"That's it. And I didn't just hand it over; they threatened me!" She was glaring at Damien.

He raised an eyebrow, scrunched up his mouth and shrugged. "They threatened you?" He couldn't imagine anyone successfully threatening Laura Troublante, but there was a first time for everything. This obviously had something to do with the Kildeer Ranch background check and mission he'd been assigned recently, but exactly what was beyond him. And at the moment, he was too sore to care.

The siren was loud now, and the patrol car pulled across the driveway, lights flashing. The officer turned off the siren, got out, and after taking in the scene, started walking their way.

"This'll take a while to explain," Damien mumbled. "Hello, officer... "

Will Weinglas and Mindy Surlees found themselves staring at each other once Troublante had raced out. Mindy's eyes were wide. What was it, fear? Anger? Will couldn't be sure.

He pushed his glasses up. "Uh, what's going on here?" he asked softly. He recognized Mindy from the previous week's reception. His reporter's instincts had picked up that something was seriously wrong.

Was Mindy trembling? Will couldn't be sure, but she was certainly troubled. And she had been arguing with Troublante when he walked in.

Mindy was trying to come to grips with what just happened. The presumed agents had certainly appeared authoritative enough, seemed to know their stuff. But now it turns out it was the Kildeers? With some sort of scheme to get a bottle of the port? If those were the Kildeers, who was the guy she hooked up with the night of the reception?

Mindy knew full well that Will was a journalist, but in the last 24 hours she'd been asked to do things that she never dreamed she'd be doing. She felt slightly sick.

"You'll have to ask Ms. Troublante when she comes back," she finally said.

Something started nagging Will at the back of his mind. It was one thing to do a puff piece on someone puffable, but something seemed sinister here. He sensed there was something going on that was much more involved than a simple winery opening. And if there **was** something going on, The Bung's cover story would make the magazine look worse than stupid, it would look duped. Of course they wouldn't report whatever it was that was going on; basically all they did was fluff. But it could mean pushing the Kildeer story to the cover.

"Mindy – you're name's Mindy, right? I think we met last Friday," he said. She nodded. "Mindy, you know that we're doing a cover story on Troublante Vineyards for the next issue. Is there any reason that you know of that we should hold the publication of that story?"

"As I said, you'll have to ask Ms. Troublante."

"OK, I guess I'll just have to wait." Will sat in one of the two chairs in front of Troublante's desk.

Mindy felt like a long day just got a little longer. "Your choice," she said, and headed back down the hall toward her own desk.

Fifteen minutes later a furious Laura Troublante walked back into her office. She saw Weinglas, and was only too ready to take out her frustrations on him, because nothing had gone right today, nothing! Not since her first year in law school had she been so thoroughly thrashed, and she was itching to get even.

Unfortunately for her, Weinglas had had time to mull over what had happened and what he had heard, and he was convinced that something was seriously amiss.

"You bring a copy of that story like I told your boss?" she snapped.

"Yeah, but after what I've seen here today, I'm not going to show it to you. You're not playing straight with us."

Troublante knew that attractive women made Wienglas a bit uneasy. Maybe I'll get some use out of this outfit today after all, she thought. She walked over to Weinglas, put one hand on the edge of her desk, and leaned forward, giving him an eyeful – had he been looking. "Where did you ever get that idea?" she said, her voice dripping disdain. "It's you who haven't been playing straight with me."

But she was about to find out she was oh-for-two today in the seduction game.

"Look, Laura, neither I nor Dudley have any desire or reason to fuck with you. Quite the opposite. Frankly, all we do is good news, so whoever called you and suggested we were putting something in the story about you screwing a judge was playing a joke on you. I really don't give a damn who you're fucking. We're a wine magazine, not a scandal sheet.

"But something is going on here today. You're meeting with Cork and Cathy Kildeer, yet you call them agents. Agents of what? You tell your hired gun to stop them. Stop them from what? They have something on you? And you're openly arguing with one of your staffers?"

Troublante had straightened up. She opened her mouth to say something ...

"Don't interrupt!" Weinglas was astonished at his own bravado, but he didn't like being played for a fool, and after getting the lay of the land was angry at his boss for not having the balls to stand up to Troublante. He pushed up his glasses: "Whatever it is that's going on here, you know what? We don't care. That's for the mainstream media. We *DO* care if a scandal is about to blow up here and it makes us look like idiots for running a positive story – a cover story no less – on you!

"I'm going to tell you straight up: the word 'sex' is not used once in our cover story, nor is the word 'judge,' nor anything else suggesting any sort of sexual activity. So as things stand now we're still going to run this story, and you'll have to accept my word that we're living up to our end of the bargain."

They stared at one another for a full minute until Troublante finally nodded and said, "OK." She instinctively knew that Weinglas was telling the truth. And she sure as hell wasn't going to tell him what had transpired in the past hour and what had precipitated it. But who would play such a prank? "If it wasn't your copy editor who called, who was it?" she asked.

Weinglas, still glaring, shook his head. "No clue."

She walked around to her side of the desk, and pressed the intercom. "Mindy, would you come in here."

Moments later, Mindy walked in, a bit more composed than when she had left. "Remember that call from the copy editor?" Troublante said. "Where did you say it came from?"

"The area code was 212, New York."

Troublante looked over at Weinglas. "You're in Chicago."

"Right," he said. "We're 312."

Suddenly it hit him: "Smythe!" he hissed.

Cork and Cathy had been waiting at Original Joe's for about 15 minutes when Bobby came strolling in. It was nearly 2 o'clock in the afternoon, and the restaurant had only a few late-lunch customers left. He slid into their booth opposite them, and whistled softly. "Fun 'n' games, kids," he grinned. Nothing seemed to faze him.

"What the hell happened?" Cork asked.

Bobby gave a full run-down. "The back half of my truck is so light that the collision just spun me around," he said. "Dented up the back side panel a bit, but otherwise, I'm fine."

A waitress brought Bobby a menu – Cork and Cathy already had theirs – and a glass of ice water. "Wait just a sec," Cork told the waitress. "We're in a bit of a hurry." He ordered the daily special – a French-dip sandwich and fries; Cathy ordered a chicken Caesar salad; and Bobby said he'd take a French-dip, too.

When the waitress had gone, Bobby continued, "The guy driving the SUV was the same guy who was pouring wine when I was there last week – Damien, I think his name is. I saw Troublante running down the driveway as I was pulling away."

"I wonder what Weinglas was doing there?" Cork mused. "I never expected to see him there."

"Bad timing or good timing, I'm not sure which," Bobby observed. "We're OK for the moment, but if they're fast, they could be waiting for us back home. So I think we better eat and run." The Kildeers agreed.

Their food orders were based on the presumption that a salad and daily specials would be served quickly, and they were right. The two men hastily ate their sandwiches, and Cathy made it halfway through her salad before saying, "I've had enough, let's go." Cork left a couple twenties on the table, and they headed to their vehicles. They still had a 2½-hour drive ahead of them.

Damien was feeling better after popping three Advils. He had come up with a transparent excuse for the cop about how he happened to crash into a block wall – he and Laura didn't dare tell what really had precipitated it. Had they implicated the other driver, whom Damien recognized and concluded was connected with the Kildeers, they felt sure their secret about the port would come to light – and that they could not risk.

The cop was skeptical; there was ample evidence that another vehicle had been involved – paint on the right corner of the SUV, a 180-degree arc in the roadway's shoulder dirt. But without the vehicle in question, and Damien's insistence that was from something else, after taking Damien's statement, the cop went on his way.

Damien was sitting on the sofa in Troublante's office; she sat on the edge of her desk, legs dangling. "So what's Plan B?" he asked.

"I think we need to make a trip to Oak Pass."

Thinking she was going to ask him to make another nighttime foray, he started to protest. "That might have worked once ..."

"No, no, I mean both of us, confront them, do whatever it takes to get that bottle back. It's not 1 yet, and if we leave now ... how long would it take us?"

Having made the drive recently, Damien said, "Five hours. If we left right this minute, it'd be 6 o'clock at the earliest before we got there, and frankly I'm just not up to driving that far today."

"I could charter an airplane; we'd be there by mid-afternoon. We could actually be there waiting for them when they got there." She leaned around and punched the intercom: "Mindy, come in here."

Moments later, Mindy walked through the door, notepad in hand. "I need to charter an airplane to take me and Damien to Oak Pass this afternoon. Call a charter service and arrange it, the faster the plane the better. And I want to leave as soon as possible."

"OK," Mindy said, and returned to her own desk. It took her awhile but she found a small charter company with a Cessna 414A willing to fly them down that afternoon for a premium. Cruising at 240 mph, it would take an hour or so to get there. Plenty of charter companies had jet service, but as soon as she mentioned the destination, they all said no can do – the Oak Pass airport's runway is too short for jets.

Will Weinglas was righteously pissed at J. Worthington Smythe. The bastard had caused him to leave the competition early, argue with The Bung's owner, Samples, and detour way out of his way to deal with Troublante. He had never had much use for Troublante, but his opinion of her had sunk even lower.

Now he needed to cool off, so after escaping the drama in the winery offices he walked over to the tasting room, anticipating that the tasting-room atmosphere and some wine would sooth his anger.

He was right. Swirling and sniffing first a merlot, then a cabernet, then a meritage, he thought about what he had just witnessed. Troublante was up to something, that was for sure. It somehow involved the Kildeers; what sort of "agents" were they posing as? If something was about to blow up, he didn't want The Bung to suffer collateral damage. It occurred to him that Troublante's assistant, Mindy, could provide a clue. I'll deal with Smythe later, he thought; now I want to find out what's going on.

He finished his wine, left the tasting room and headed back across the lobby toward the business offices. He saw Troublante and Damien walking hurriedly across the parking lot toward a car. Good, he thought; I'll take another crack at Mindy. Maybe I can get her to tell me what's happening.

Mindy sat at her desk, numb from all that had happened. She was now involved in a criminal conspiracy; she was exhausted; and she was miserable.

She heard the door open and looked up to see Will Weinglas, the guy whose glasses always seemed to be slipping down his nose. She had no energy to even smile at him; she just stared.

"I was hoping I'd find you still here," Will said. She didn't respond.

"I want to know what's going on. Mysterious agents, the Kildeers, your boss and her hatchet man racing out of here. What's the story?"

It was too much. A sob involuntarily welled up and burst from Mindy's mouth; tears coursed down her cheeks as she raised her hands to her face in an effort to hide her embarrassment, her misery apparent.

Will pulled one of the chairs to the front of Mindy's desk and sat down, sympathetic to her distress. Softly he said, "Please tell me."

Mindy struggled to control her emotions: "It's a long story," she said.

"I've got time." He smiled. She seemed to be a nice person caught in bad situation.

Mindy was torn. Part of her wanted to tell the world what a bitch Laura Troublante was, but the other part realized that doing so would reveal her own vulnerability in this growing debacle. Plus, Mindy was still an employee. And even though The Bung was soft news, she recognized that Weinglas was a reporter, and reporters revealed things. "Let's just say Ms. Troublante's day isn't going as expected."

"I can see that for myself. Tell me something I don't know."

"You're a smart guy; you'll figure it out."

"Where'd she go in such a hurry?" He glanced at her notepad. She saw where he was looking and covered it up – too late. He looked up at her. "Oak Pass? That's where the Kildeers live." He paused. "They were carrying a bottle when they left. What was it?"

"I don't know."

She was unconvincing. "More like you won't tell me. OK. Let's see ... the Kildeers are here posing as some sort of agents. They leave with a bottle. Your boss doesn't know they're the Kildeers until I get here, then goes tearing after them, and now is going to Oak Pass to confront them. They must have something on her, some leverage. How'm I doing so far?"

"Like I said, you're a smart guy."

"So like I asked Ms. Troublante, whatever is going on between her and the Kildeers – will it affect the story we have on Troublante Vineyards?"

"I don't know, and frankly I don't want to know. I don't know what your story says, and I don't want to speculate. Really, I can't tell you anything."

"OK, fair enough. I gotta tell you though, you look like a nice person, so I can't figure out why you'd want to work for a witch like Laura Troublante. If I were in your shoes, I'd be dusting off my resume."

She looked at him with haunted eyes. "That's probably good advice."

Will got up to leave. He reached into his pocket and pulled out his business card and handed it to Mindy. "If you change your mind, gimme a call."

Mindy looked at it, then back at Will. "I don't think I will, but thanks."

Johnny Yaw's internal radar detected what appeared to be trouble. A power couple if ever he had seen one had just climbed out of a Cessna 414 at the Oak Pass airport coming in from Napa and rushed up to the general aviation desk, where young Johnny was holding down the fort. It wasn't so much what they had asked but how they asked it that alarmed him.

Some iron-pumping muscle-bound guy and a woman who looked like, well, she was used to getting her way, wanted directions to the rental car agency and to Kildeer Ranch. The past couple weeks had seen others arrive at the airport with identical questions, only they seemed happy and excited about the prospect of finding a rare wine. This couple – the woman in particular – had an intensity about them; they were on a mission. They clearly weren't the law, but something didn't seem right.

After answering their questions and watching them race off to the car-rental counter, Johnny sat for a minute before making up his mind. Oak Pass was a small town, and people looked out for one another here. He picked up the phone and called Boobsie's.

Millie answered on the first ring. "Hi Mizz Bounty, it's Johnny out at the airport."

"Hi, Johnny! How's everything? Your folks doin' OK? Haven't seen 'em in a couple weeks."

"They're fine, Mizz Bounty. I'll tell 'em you said hi."

"So what's going on, Johnny? How can I help you?"

"Well, I don't know, Mizz Bounty, but something kinda strange just happened, and I don't know... I thought I should let someone know."

"What is it, honey? What happened?"

Johnny related how the intense couple had come in looking for Kildeer Ranch. Millie listened intently. "Describe them for me, Johnny." He did. His description didn't fit anyone she knew, but like Johnny, her radar was on full alert.

"Thanks, Johnny, I'll let you know what I find out."

She hung up, and drummed her fingers on the counter for a couple seconds. Then she dialed Travis Ellis.

"Hi, TR, it's Millie. I think trouble just showed up in Oak Pass."

"Oh? What kind of trouble?"

"A woman and a man just flew into town and asked Johnny Yaw directions to Kildeer Ranch."

"What's unusual about that?"

"I'm not sure," Millie said. "But something about them didn't set right with Johnny. You mind picking me up and we take a ride out to Kildeers?"

"Be there asap," Travis said.

Driving 80-plus miles per hour will shave time off a trip, and Cork, Cathy and Bobby were only about 10 minutes north of Oak Pass at 4:30. Bobby took a cut off that Cork and Cathy knew went to his place. Cork raised his hand out the window and Bobby returned the wave. He'd be by later, they knew.

His memory refreshed by the kid's directions at the airport, Damien had no problem finding Kildeer Ranch again. There were still cars in the parking area, when he and Laura drove up at a quarter to 5. They parked and as they were getting out, a little white car that looked familiar pulled into the driveway.

Cork and Cathy had seen the car pull into their driveway just before they did, and didn't think anything of it until they were turning into the driveway themselves and saw the couple getting out of the car.

"Oh my God!" Cathy blurted out, her hand coming to her mouth involuntarily.

"Shit!" Cork said.

They drove up and parked in front of their house, and sat for a moment, staring at Laura and Damien. A smile had spread over Laura Troublante's face.

Without saying a word, Cork and Cathy got out of the car and started walking toward Troublante.

Travis and Millie were about a half a mile behind Cork and Cathy, and saw the little white car pull into the

Kildeer Ranch driveway; they slowed and pulled into the driveway. In front of them they saw Cork and Cathy walking toward another couple.

"Who's that," Millie asked.

"That's Laura Troublante," Travis said. "I think you were right about trouble showing up here."

When Cork and Cathy had gotten within about 20 feet of Laura and Damien they stopped. "The shoe's on the other foot now," Troublante said, venom dripping with each word. "You have something of mine. I want it back."

"Sorry, Laura, but it's the price for what you've already taken," Cork said.

"I've taken? What have I taken from you?"

"I recognize your gigolo there. He and I met a few days ago in my winery. Only it was after hours and he was draining my tanks. That's a few thousand dollars you cost me, not to mention the medical attention. So I think a bottle of phony port is more than fair."

"Damien?" Troublante said softly. Damien stepped forward, even with Troublante. The look on his face said he was looking forward to a confrontation.

"Now I'd prefer not to cause trouble here," Troublante continued, "but that bottle belongs to me, and I intend to leave with it regardless of how I get it." Her voice was threatening.

"Your intentions are of no concern to me," Cork said. "As I said, you owe me for what you already took. The 'port' is the price. Now I'm going to ask you to get off my property." He was mentally preparing to engage Damien.

"I said I didn't want trouble..."

"Then don't cause it." The voice came from behind her; Troublante whirled around to see who was challenging her. She hadn't heard anyone approaching but there were two people, and she knew one of them: Travis Ellis, a local vintner.

"You don't want any trouble, and frankly neither do we, so why stir it up?" Ellis said. His words were congenial, but his physical presence was menacing.

"But if you want to make trouble, you came to the right place," said the bounteous woman standing next to Ellis. Troublante stared at her; was that a smile on her face? She looked as if she was actually hoping something would start.

Cork and Cathy were bolstered by the unexpected rear-guard action provided by TR and Millie. "The so-called port is staying right here," Cork said. "It's our insurance policy. You leave us alone, and the port stays put. Oh, and drop that bogus lawsuit. But if your pal here, or you, or anyone else that we remotely suspect is connected to you causes us any problems – so much as a leaky faucet – the BATF will get a chance to examine the contents of that bottle."

Troublante recognized that the odds had shifted. If she couldn't get the bottle back, there were no guarantees. She didn't like not being in control. "I don't trust you," Troublante said.

"Well we sure as hell don't trust you!" Cathy practically screamed. "Look what you've done to us! And for what? Your own damned ego?"

Cork looked askance at his wife; she rarely, if ever, swore. She must be really upset, he thought.

"You think you can have whatever you want without so much as lifting a finger," Cathy continued. "You just buy it. Buy your way into the wine business. Buy your friends. You try and buy a vineyard that's been cared for and nurtured for nearly a century and take credit for it, just like that. Well, it's not yours, and it never will be yours! So just ... just ..." she was so mad she was red in the face, "just go fuck yourself!"

Bobby had stopped at his place to check on things, but was quickly headed to Kildeer Ranch. A few minutes later, as he was approaching the turn-in to his friends' winery, he noticed that his brake pedal was going almost to the floor. His truck slowed barely enough to make the turn. What the hell? he mused. As he drove up the driveway he suddenly saw in front of him what appeared to be a confrontation. There was Cork and Cathy, and on the right, were Travis and Millie. And directly in front of him was ... No! It couldn't be! Was that Laura Troublante and her hired muscle?

He put his foot on the brake pedal and pressed down – all the way to floor. He pumped the brake pedal! Nothing. He had no brakes! And he was traveling at about 25 miles per hour toward six people!

He slammed his automatic gearshift into the lowest gear, the engine revved loudly as it was forced by the lower gear into much higher revolutions, slowing the truck.

Travis and Millie heard the engine noise and turned to see Bobby and his truck less than 50 feet away and closing fast. Travis grabbed Millie's arm and jumped out of the way. Cork and Cathy also scrambled out of the way.

Even though the truck was slowing, it was still moving fairly quickly directly toward Laura and Damien, who seemed frozen. At the last second, Damien jumped to the side. Laura started to move but was too late.

Bobby was looking to see which way he could turn to avoid hitting anyone, and spun the steering wheel hard left. Even as it slowed, the truck had momentum. The back end came loose and the truck broadsided Laura just as she started to move.

It was like a giant hand slapped her and she was knocked back several feet, landing on her rear. The truck slid by and came to rest against Troublante's rental car. The impact did little damage to either vehicle. Bobby, still gripping the steering wheel, jammed the gearshift into park and switched off the ignition, glad to be stopped.

Laura found herself on her back in the gravel, dust swirling around. She tried to sit up, but found she was just one giant ache. Jesus! she thought. Is this vineyard really worth it?

Damien, unscathed, rushed over to her. "Are you OK?" he said. She looked up at him and said, "I think so, but shit! Everything hurts." She sat in the dirt with her legs sticking straight out. She shook her aching head, and groaned. Finally, she extended her right hand slowly and asked Damien to help her up.

Cork, Cathy, Travis and Millie had come over and were standing nearby. Bobby was standing behind them. Laura recognized him immediately. "You!" she exclaimed. "You told me you were Cork Kildeer!"

"I did no such thing," Bobby grinned. "Your gal gave me that nametag and you assumed that's who I was. I thought it was kinda funny, so I didn't say jack shit."

"I ought to sue you!" she said.

"For what?" Bobby said. "Your own stupidity?"

"And that would be one of those problems we mentioned earlier that will get you face to face with the good folks at the BATF," Cork interjected. Then he laughed. "You want to talk lawsuits? Maybe I should sue you for willful destruction of private property."

She glared at him. These Goddamned wine people! Why couldn't they just accept her? Wasn't it just one big country club anyway? She had the initiation fee – her palatial winery's cost should have been more than enough – so why did they resist her? Why couldn't she have what she wanted? Why didn't they respect her?

"Why won't you sell me your winery?" she blurted out in pure frustration. "You'll be set financially for the rest of your life! I don't understand you!"

"And you never will," Cork said. "You earn respect, you don't buy it. My family has owned and worked this land for more than half a century. We've returned to the soil what we've taken. We've nurtured and nourished it. We're one with the land. And now you think you can just come in and buy 60 some years' worth of TLC? You wouldn't have a clue what to do."

"Here's what I suggest," Millie chimed in. "Go on back where you came from, and instead of trying to buy respect, start earning it. I know all about your kind; seen a few of you in my time."

"Laura," Travis said, "let's turn your question around. Why do *you* want to buy this winery?

Before she could say anything, he continued: "Let me answer it for you: the only reason you want it is you think it'll give you a hundred-point wine. You're dying for relevance, but you have no idea what goes into making good wine. It's not just the grapes. It's the winemaker's skill, the vineyard manager's skill, Mother Nature – so many small things. It's not just about money. It's about investing time and effort to learn the science *and* the art. You don't want to bother with all that.

"But these kids do. They've put in the time and effort. And that's why they got a hundred-point score."

Laura's shoulders sagged. They had her over a barrel, she realized. And, with the faux port in their hands, they also had leverage. No bullshitting her way out. She looked away. She was not used to losing. And she recognized she had just lost.

She was forced to look at the practical aspect of the situation: was it worth continuing the effort? The answer, she had to admit, was no. Why waste further time on something that had already cost her way too much time and money? Piss on it. Her pride, dignity – even her dress – was in tatters.

And so was her resolve to acquire Kildeer Ranch. There were other vineyards she could acquire; she'd get that hundred from Smythe some other way.

She looked at Travis, a dull ache throbbing in her head. "Fuck you," she said. "Fuck all of you! C'mon, Damien, let's go. I hate these fucking people."

"Don't come back," said Bobby.

"Yeah, we're not what you'd call a 'friendly port,'" Cork chimed in and grinned.

Travis and Millie glanced at him, raising their eyebrows. Cathy looked at her husband, mouth open, not believing what he just said. Bobby smiled and shook his head. And Damien actually looked back and winked at Cork.

Glaring, Laura gave him the bird before turning on her heel and marching to her rental car. She and Damian climbed in, backed it away from Bobby's truck, and spun the tires in the dirt, raising a dust cloud all the way down the driveway.

Cork and Cathy stood looking after them. A smile formed on Cork's face. He slowly turned his head and looked at Cathy, who was also smiling. Just then Travis clapped Cork on the shoulder, and Millie put her arm around Cathy.

"Kids," Millie said, "I think you did it!"

Added Bobby: "I think you did, too!"

"I think it's time to fire up the grill," said Travis. "Everybody come on out to my place. And you two, bring some of that damn zin. It's caused so much trouble, we better drink some of it."

Chapter 13

FRIDAY & SATURDAY, APRIL 22-23

Will Weinglas headed to San Francisco after leaving Troublante Vineyards, glad that he'd reserved a seat on that redeye back to Chicago. After calling Samples to let him know he'd be in the office the next day, he'd left Troublante around 2. He decided to stop in San Francisco for a few hours before catching his flight. He was in The City a little after 3; he parked near Union Square and caught a cable car over to Fishermen's Wharf.

Since it was early, he had no trouble getting a seat at one of the seafood restaurants overlooking the harbor, enjoying a glass of wine and some fresh local catch for dinner. With nothing better to do, he made his way back to his rental car. At 7 p.m., rush hour was mostly over, and he had little trouble getting to the airport. By 9, he had turned in his car, obtained his boarding pass, found his departure gate and was settling in for the wait until takeoff. He was exhausted, and glad for the time to be able to think about what had happened.

What a damn day! He kept wondering about what he'd stumbled on – the intrigue with the Kildeers and Troublante; the assistant, Mindy, looked like she'd been on the losing end of a brawl; Troublante going berserk. Damn Laura Troublante! He frankly didn't care if he ever saw her again.

Then there was Smythe. That son of a bitch! That bastard was the reason he'd had such a miserable day. What Smythe had done was way over the top. Over the course of several days Smythe's collective sins had added up to a serious indictment: he'd spilled wine all over Will's shirt, acted like an insufferable snob at that restaurant (Will chuckled at the memory of Smythe sampling urine), then orchestrated some prank that had Will racing nearly the length of California to put out an imaginary fire.

Well, thought Will, you're no better than anyone else, you pompous prick. How could he get Smythe's nose back down to the same level as everyone else's? Hmmm…

An idea started to take shape. Doesn't Dudley have a top-end copy machine? And what was the name of that weathercaster in New York? She was a Bung subscriber and had once emailed Will about a story he'd written. What was her name…

By the time he boarded, his plan had started taking shape. The plane was only about half full, so he was able to find a row to himself. He fell asleep shortly after takeoff and slept soundly until just before landing at 5:30 a.m. in Chicago.

Shortly after 9 a.m., Will walked into The Bung offices. He headed over to Samples' desk and sat down. It was Saturday morning, and only one other staffer was in the office. Dud was on his second cup of coffee.

"So how'd it go?" Samples asked hopefully.

"Pretty damn bad, Dud, we were duped. The whole thing was Smythe."

"What do you mean? How'd Smythe get involved?"

"It was all him from the start. He had someone call Troublante posing as one of our copy editors, stirring up trouble. Laura of course took the bait and raised hell with you. As a result I went on a wild goose chase. And there's something else going on there."

He related how he'd encountered the Kildeers when he arrived and the frantic effort to stop them. He also described his own conversation with Troublante, his refusal to show her the story, and her eventual acquiescence.

"Dud, I'm telling you – no, pleading with you – we should really rethink making the Troublante story the cover. There's something going on there that I don't like. I don't know what it is, but it smells like three-day-old fish."

Samples, though, was still concerned about losing Troublante's advertising. "A deal's a deal," he said. "It'll only get worse if we don't give her the cover. Besides, her wine's not *that* bad."

"No, it's not," Will conceded. "But it's not great, either. At least tease from the cover to the Kildeer story. That way we're covered and don't look like complete idiots. We can also run the Kildeer story closer to the front, which will give it more of a news play than a feature play. We can give the Troublante story the double truck, which ought to make Laura happy."

Samples looked thoughtful for a couple seconds, then, recognizing Will's logic, nodded his agreement. "OK, we can do that."

"Whew! Thank you!" Will said, relief evident in his voice. Then, "I need to make a couple calls. And I'm going to New York in a couple of days."

"What's going on there?"

"If I told you I'd have to kill you," Will said, laughing. "But I think you'll like the outcome, if I can pull it off."

"Say no more," Samples said with the beginning of a smile. "I assume it has something to do with Smythe?"

Weinglas raised his hand and looked away with a mischievous grin.

Stormy Knight was pleasantly surprised to get an email from Will Weinglas. He was coming to town to conduct research on the Big Apple's wine bars for an upcoming article in The Bung. Would she like to get together for a glass of wine and discuss a project he had in mind?

Would she? Of course! The weathercaster at WINE-TV coincidentally enjoyed the very beverage spelled by the station's call letters, and was a loyal Bung reader. She was happy that Will remembered her. She emailed back that she'd be delighted to meet with him – anything to help with the story. In fact, she was familiar with a few wine bars in Manhattan and would be happy to show them to him. After a couple of exchanges, they were able to set a date.

Chapter 14

MONDAY, APRIL 25

Two days later at about 7:20 p.m., Stormy walked into the bar of a restaurant two blocks from the station and found Will waiting for her.

He pushed up his glasses as she approached, and stood to greet her. "Miss Knight? Hi, I'm Will Weinglas from The Wine Bung. Nice to actually meet you. Thanks for meeting with me." He extended his hand.

"Nice to meet you, too, Will!" she said enthusiastically as they shook hands. "Please, I'm Stormy. I only got interested in wine a couple years ago, and your stories have helped me understand it better. So thank *you!*"

"You're more than welcome. I'm glad they've helped. And I'd like to help that understanding with a glass of wine. You're off the rest of night, right?"

"Yep, sure am."

"What are you in the mood for? Red? White?"

"I'm thinking white," she said.

"Terrific! They have a delightful sauvignon blanc on the wine list here that I'd like you to try."

"Fabulous!"

Will ordered a bottle; after the server had opened and poured for them, Will offered a toast: "Cheers!" and each sipped.

"So what's the project you mentioned," Knight asked.

"Stormy, have you heard of a guy named J. Worthington Smythe? He lives here in New York City. Publishes a wine newsletter."

She looked thoughtful, then slowly said, "Yeah ... I've heard of his newsletter, but I haven't read it. I've never met him."

"Do you ever do live-remotes during the newscast?"

"Yeah, sometimes. Now that the weather's warming up we're doing a few."

"Do you ever have guests on during the live-remotes?"

"Once in awhile," she replied, a smile starting to form as she picked up Will's conspiratorial tone. "Why? What do you have in mind?"

Chapter 15

TUESDAY, APRIL 26

Josephine was excited when she walked into J. Worthington Smythe's office. "WINE-TV is on the line," she said. "They want you for a promo on an upcoming newscast."

"Really," Smythe said, raising an eyebrow. But whom else would they call, he thought. He picked up the phone, flattered that a TV station had sought out his expertise.

"J. Worthington Smythe here," he said.

"Good morning, Mr. Smythe, my name's Jacqui Smith. Our names are almost the same." She giggled. Oh, one of those, Smythe thought, his annoyance rising.

"How can I help you," he intoned coldly, ignoring the name comparison.

Jacqui Smith quickly ascertained Smythe's attitude and got right to the point. "We're planning a live-remote broadcast during the weather segments on an upcoming newscast. The forecast for the next week to 10 days is nice, spring weather, and our weathercaster, Stormy Knight, wanted to feature al fresco wine tasting as a way to focus on the pleasant spring. She said you wrote a wine newsletter, and wondered if you would be willing to come on the show to offer your expertise."

WINE-TV had a huge viewership in the Greater New York area. It almost instantly occurred to Smythe that this was a chance for some major self-promotion. "Yes, of course," he said. "I'd be delighted."

Smith described a restaurant with an outdoor dining area, Chaud Poulette. "Are you familiar with the place?"

In fact, Smythe was quite familiar with the place. The restaurant's owner proclaimed a love of all things French but in fact had never been to France. His poor grasp of the language was most evident in the restaurant's name, a lost-in-translation effort. He had wanted the name to reflect attractive young women, thinking it suggested a restaurant with attractive, imaginative cuisine. *Belles Filles* might have worked. Instead he came up with *Chaud Poulette*: hot young chickens. Somehow the name had stuck.

"Yes, I know Chaud Poulette," Smythe intoned. "An excellent wine list; an excellent choice for a venue."

Jacqui Smith gave him the date two days hence. "Could you be there at 4:45? The remote crew will arrive at 4 to set up, and the newscast begins at 5. The first weather segment will occur at 5:07. You'll be introduced as the renowned wine expert you are, then at 5:15, you'll be interviewed briefly before the main weathercast. We'd like you to taste a wine and offer your opinion. Will that work for you?"

These Philistines, Smythe thought, child's play. But he said: "Of course; I'll be there."

Chapter 16

THURSDAY, APRIL 28

Will dropped by the TV station shortly after 1 p.m., and asked for Stormy. When she came to the lobby, he handed her a brown paper wine-bag with a bottle of wine.

"Your prop," he said with a grin.

Stormy pulled out the bottle. They both chuckled. "This will be great," she said.

Smythe arrived at Chaud Poulette promptly at 4:45. The crew was set up; a van with a 30-foot extended transmitting antenna was parked at the curb with black cables running to the camera mounted on a tripod and small TV-set on the ground by the camera. A smaller cable was attached to a hand-held microphone.

A young woman with shoulder-length black hair wearing a form-fitting sweater and skirt about four inches above the knee was talking with a casually dressed man standing by the recording camera on a tripod. They were standing by a round table inside the railing separating the outdoor dining area from the sidewalk. The table was covered with a white tablecloth; on the table was a red carnation in a vase, a Riedel Bordeaux wine glass and a corkscrew.

Stormy saw Smythe standing a few feet away, and walked over extending her hand. "Mr. Smythe? So good to meet you! Thank you for coming on the show. I've just started getting into wine myself, so I'm delighted to meet someone so knowledgeable."

"Well, yes, of course, but who else could you possibly have asked?" Smythe smirked.

"Exactly!" Stormy's face lit up with a dazzling smile, but she was thinking, Gawd! What a pompous ass.

"Mr. Smythe, the newscast begins at 5; you can watch what's happening at the station on the monitor down there" – she motioned to the small TV-set on the ground by the tripod. "At 5:07 they'll segue to us; I'll have you standing here by me. I'll talk a little about the weather, and tell our viewers that we'll be talking with you in just a few minutes during the main weathercast. You won't have to be mic'd-up; I'll use the hand-held microphone."

"Excellent!" Smythe said. "No problem."

At 5 p.m. the newscast began. Stormy slipped on a blue blazer with the station's logo on the breast pocket. The anchors were delivering the main news. Stormy had an earpiece, as did the cameraman. They could see on the small monitor as the anchors were saying, "... and now our chief meteorologist, Stormy Knight, has a special guest tonight to help us celebrate this beautiful spring weather. Stormy?"

"That's right, Bill. And it *is* a beautiful day here in the Big Apple, with temperatures still around 80 degrees under blue skies. It's a perfect day to get out and enjoy some fruit of the vine, shall we say, and joining us is renowned wine critic and New York resident J. Worthington Smythe, publisher of Wines by Smythe."

She turned slightly and gestured to Smythe, who had a foolish looking grin staring straight into the camera. If he looked a bit stiff, that's because he was; despite his stature he was not used to appearing on television and was uneasy.

"We'll be showcasing his vast knowledge in just a few minutes when we return with the full forecast, but now Bill, back to you in the studio."

The anchors picked up the dialogue, moving into a 2½-minute commercial stretch.

As soon as she was off camera, Stormy turned to Smythe and said, "Just stay here for a minute, I'll be right back." She winked at him as she picked up the corkscrew and moved into the restaurant. Once inside she picked up the bottle that Will had given her earlier that afternoon. She had taped the brown paper bag around the bottle's neck. Using the corkscrew she pulled the cork, then took the bottle back out to the sidewalk table, where she put both the corkscrew and the bagged bottle.

The anchors were just returning to news reading; Smythe looked at the bottle and smiled. Knight was going to test his skills. He wasn't worried; after all, he could identify most Bordeaux classified growths by year and vineyard. He could identify many California wines and their vintage, including most of the major brands from Napa Valley. What could go wrong?

Stormy turned to Smythe. "OK, Mr. Smythe, this time I'm going to have you stand a few feet over here off camera, and then I'll bring you into the shot, like a big introduction; I'll motion you in."

The live-remote broadcast had attracted quite a crowd – passers-by, wine fans, TV junkies – and they were excited to see Smythe in action.

The anchors were preparing to pass the baton: "... Stormy Knight is at the popular French bistro Chaud Poulette with a certain celebrity. What's happening there, Stormy?"

Stormy was right on cue: "Hi Bill, it's a beautiful evening here, a great evening to get out and enjoy some wine, and to help us with that is the renowned wine critic J. Worthington Smythe." She motioned Smythe over, and he stepped into the shot.

"J. Worthington has such a reputation for being able to identify wines that we're going to demonstrate his fabulous prowess right here. Are you ready, J. Worthington?"

Smythe again grinned awkwardly at the camera and said, "Yes, Miss Knight, bring it on." He had already discerned by the shape of the bagged bottle that it was likely a cabernet or sauvignon blanc, something like that, since the bottle had square shoulders.

"OK, then, here we go. I'm pouring J. Worthington a taste from our special bottle, for him to identify it for us."

She tipped the bottle up and poured a couple ounces. Smythe was startled to see the wine was light pink; he had not expected pink wine. A rosé, he thought; OK, no problem.

He picked up the glass and swirled the wine, lifting it to his nose. The only aroma he got was … grapey? He lifted the glass to his lips and tasted. Slightly sweet, no discernable varietal character. What the hell was it? Fear started to gnaw at him. He tasted it again, but … nothing!

Had he spent any time on the wine judging circuit, he would have recognized white zinfandel almost immediately. But he had never been to a wine competition, and he had never tried white zinfandel.

"I … I…"

"J. Worthington, it's one of the most popular wines in America," Stormy said. She tilted her head and smiled some encouragement.

"Uh… I…"

Time was up; Stormy had to move on. "Oh my! We've stumped the great J. Worthington Smythe!"

The crowd went, "Ahhh!" Some started laughing. Hard to believe the great Smythe couldn't guess something so simple.

"I really thought this would be too easy for you. We even had the wine custom labeled just for you to commemorate the occasion." She was tearing the bag open and pulled out the bottle. "It reads:

'Especially bottled for
J. Worthington Smythe
Big Valley, California
White Zinfandel.'

"Thank you so much, Mr. Smythe for coming on today and being such a good sport."

Smythe was humiliated. Here on live television in the nation's largest TV market he had been tripped up. He just stood there feeling like his face was on fire, looking out at the crowd – Knight was by now into the actual weather forecast – when suddenly ... who was that?!? He thought he saw a familiar face; the man was looking right at him with a slight smile. Then he pushed up his glasses. Weinglas!! That son of a bitch! He's behind this! How the hell...

The face had vanished.

Chapter 17

TUESDAY, MAY 9

Millie Bounty smiled broadly as she saw who was coming in the door of Boobsies.

"Cork and Cathy! Great to see you kids! How's everything?"

The proprietors of Kildeer Ranch Winery smiled in response and each gave Millie a hug. "We're doing great, Millie," Cork said. "I think things are pretty much back to normal."

"We're almost sold out of the 100-point wine," Cathy chimed in. "We think the next vintage is almost as good, so we'll see how that goes. We'll bottle it soon. We'll have to with the demand."

"Looks like you've pretty well recovered from your recent ordeal, none the worse for wear, anyway," Millie smiled.

"Yeah, things have quieted down," Cork replied. "And we haven't heard from Laura Troublante since that day at our place."

About then, Millie saw a familiar pickup pull into her parking lot and find a spot. Bobby Vangree got out of the driver's side, and a young woman Millie didn't recognize got out of the passenger side. "Now who do you suppose that is with Bobby," she said.

Cork and Cathy turned to see, and both recognized Mindy Surlees. "You've got to be kidding me!" Cathy said.

"That's Mindy, Laura Troublante's assistant," Cork said, alarm in his voice. "Maybe I spoke too soon."

A few seconds later the door opened and a grinning Bobby and a shy Mindy walked in.

"Hi, guys!" Bobby blurted out. "I think you two met Mindy."

"Uh, yeah, we have," Cork said, looking curiously at Mindy. Cathy had one eyebrow raised. They glanced at each another, both thinking that perhaps they hadn't heard the last of Laura Troublante.

A momentary awkward silence descended, before Millie stepped up.

"Well I haven't met her," Millie said. "Hi, I'm Millie; I run this place. Anyone who's a friend of these three is welcome here." She and Mindy shook hands. Mindy smiled at the warm welcome.

"It's nice to meet you, Millie. My name's Mindy, Mindy Surlees."

"These two said you work for Laura Troublante?" Millie said, pointing her thumb toward Cork and Cathy.

"Used to," Mindy said. "I left last week."

"Oh?" Cork and Cathy said in unison.

"I think you kids should sit down over here," Millie said, gesturing to a large table. "The lunch rush is over, and I'm going to join you to hear what's going on. Rhonda?" She gestured to one of the servers. "Could you get these kids some menus and something to drink?"

"Sure thing!" Rhonda replied cheerfully. "What can I get you?" After taking their drink orders, she returned a couple minutes later with two iced teas and two sodas, ice water for Millie and four menus.

Cathy couldn't contain herself any longer. "I'm a little confused. Last time we saw you was at Troublante Vineyards. Now you come in with Bobby and say you left Troublante. OK, so tell us. What is going on?"

"Guys, lemme explain," Bobby interjected. "You remember when I first went up there to the reception?

Well, I met Mindy. She was the greeter there, and gave me a tour of the place. She was the one who told me about the port.

"Well, we went out to dinner that night and got to know each other better, and I felt kinda bad that I hadn't been able to tell her who I really was, ya know? So after the whole deal was over, I went back up there to set the record straight. I felt I owed her that much."

They all nodded and waited.

"And besides, I really like her." He turned and grinned at Mindy, winking at her. She smiled and blushed.

"You, Bobby?" Cork said. "You actually like someone enough to drive up to Napa and bring her back to Oak Pass? You actually like someone well enough to spend more than one night with her?" Cork was smiling.

"Well ... you know ..." Bobby squirmed, grinning and blushing. He knew Cork was teasing. "I just knew there was something more to Mindy than meets the eye, and I wanted to get to know her as me, not you."

"I'm glad you did," Mindy said. "After the big blowup at the winery, I wondered who that was that I went out with."

They all laughed a bit at that.

"So what happened at Troublante?" Cathy reiterated.

"I couldn't stand working there anymore," Mindy said. "There were things going on there that I didn't feel right about. When Laura got the call from that BATF agent, she made me hide all the port in my garage. I felt like I was being dragged into something illegal and sleazy. She just gave me no choice, and I don't want to work for someone like that."

Millie leaned over and put a hand on Mindy's arm. "Honey, I was the BATF agent," she said with a grin.

"Oh my gosh!" Mindy said, shaking her head. They all laughed.

"So what's happening with Laura?" Cork asked.

"I'm not really sure," Mindy said. "When she got back to the winery, she was a lot bitchier than normal for a couple days. A couple guys from the winery came and got the port out of my garage and took it back. I have no idea what she's going to do with it, but I'm pretty sure she's not going to try and sell it.

"The Bung story came out with Troublante Vineyards on the cover, so that helped calm her down. But I don't know what she's going to do next and I don't care. I just wanted out."

She smiled slightly, and looked at Cork and Cathy. "I also noticed a nice little blurb on the cover about you guys." Weinglas, in his story about Kildeer Ranch, had scored their wine a 99. Of course, he couldn't give them the same score Smythe had, but a 99 was virtually as rare as 100.

Sharing what she knew seemed therapeutic, and her frustrations overflowed. "She's always gotten whatever she wanted, one way or another, and is still licking her wounds, so to speak. I think encountering you, Cathy, really threw her for a loop. She manipulates men, and anticipated that the agents would be men, so when you walked in and started telling her how things were going to be, it caught her totally off guard."

"She seemed completely frustrated when she and – what's the guy's name that was with her?" Cathy asked.

"Damien."

"Yeah, when she and Damien came here. She couldn't understand why we wouldn't sell to her."

"She thinks money can buy anything, and all anyone cares about is money. I actually think she's a sociopath."

"So where does this leave you, Mindy?"

"I don't know yet. When I told her I was quitting, she just shrugged, told me to wait for a few minutes while she prepared my final check. It was like she knew I was going to leave. The moment I walked out the door, I felt like a huge weight had been lifted off my shoulders.

"When I got my degree I planned on being an elementary school teacher. But I like the wine industry. I mean, I grew up in a town where that's the main industry, so it's not something that's a mystery to me. I've enjoyed the people I've met, and I did learn a lot when I was working for Laura. Then this guy came along" – she gestured at Bobby – "and he's a whole lot more fun, so I think I'll hang out with him awhile and see where that takes me."

"So how did you reconnect?" Cathy asked.

"It was actually the day I quit. I had just gotten my final check and was leaving the office. As I went into the foyer, Bobby was standing there. He said hi and that he was there to see me. I said, well, you're not Cork Kildeer, so who the hell are you? He said that's what he wanted to talk to me about. He took me to lunch and told me the whole story from your end."

"Talk about luck," said Bobby. "The day I go up there is the day she's quitting, and I catch her as she's walking out. I'd have found her eventually but it would have taken longer."

Mindy turned toward Cork and Cathy. "I'm really sorry you had to go through all that, and I'm sorry for any part I may have played in it. I'm really happy for you and your scores from Smythe and The Bung."

"Don't even worry about it, Mindy," Cork said warmly. "If it weren't for you, things wouldn't have turned out nearly as well as they did. And besides, look at this guy you've hooked up with. What a bonus!" He slapped Bobby on the back and laughed. Bobby just grinned.

"You could do a lot worse!" Millie said. "All these kids are great. And I can see you are, too, Mindy. So lemme get Rhonda over here to get you fed. Mindy, you're going to fit right in here in Oak Pass."

Epilogue

- Cork and Cathy Kildeer continued to farm their vineyard, selling some of their grapes, and using the best lots for their wine. Their zinfandel continued to garner critical acclaim. They adhered to their friend Bobby's advice and kept the price of their wine at $50. It didn't slow sales at all. And they never saw Laura Troublante again.

- Bobby Vangree and Mindy Surlees' relationship blossomed. Eventually she moved in with him, and the two of them continue to work on building up Clover Leaf Cellars. Some of their grapes come from Kildeer Ranch, but they've never gotten a 100 point score.

- Dudley Samples and Will Weinglas continued sparring with J. Worthington Smythe. Smythe insisted that The Wine Bung was just a shill for the wine industry, while Samples and Weinglas opined that Smythe was an arrogant snob. There was likely some truth in both views.

- Millie Bounty still runs The Boobsie Twins and supports Oak Pass youth fundraising efforts. She managed to get a beer-and-wine license and now has a nice wine list featuring local wines, including Clover Leaf Cellars and T.R. Ellis Winery. She pairs her famous burgers with Kildeer Ranch Zinfandel.

• Damien saw the handwriting on the wall and hit the road shortly after Mindy quit Troublante Vineyards. His whereabouts are unknown.

• Laura Troublante never did acquire any more vineyard land, and she never bothered the Kildeers again, dropping the nuisance suit she'd filed. Her sales never seemed to gain traction. Following an initial flurry of interest after The Bung story was published, business returned to its previous level, perhaps even a little less. A couple months after The Bung story came out, a real BATF agent showed up for a spot inspection. Troublante, thinking it was another trick, treated the agent so rudely that the agent ran everyone out of the tasting room and slapped a chain and padlock on the doors, promising to have a team of accountants go over Troublante Vineyards' books. Before that could happen, Troublante said enough is enough. She closed Troublante Vineyards and returned to her former profession. The last anyone knew, the winery was still for sale.

Zinforado! Acknowledgements

This is a work of fiction. And as with any work of fiction, there are a number of people to whom I owe thanks, who helped me whether they realized it or not. Over the years the friends I've made in the wine business have shared their experiences, and many of those experiences are quite funny. I've incorporated some of those tales here.

The characters in this book are fictional, products of my imagination, though readers may recognize real people who inspired them. The characters are composites drawn from many people with whom I've crossed paths and are not intended to reflect any particular person. Any such reflection is purely coincidental.

For the technical aspects of winemaking I consulted with many people who freely shared their expertise and insider knowledge. This has allowed me to, I hope, accurately portray the wine industry. It's a fun, funny, stimulating, exciting and political landscape, one that I've enjoyed being part of.

Thank you so much to all of you who have answered my questions and helped me gain a greater understanding and appreciation for a beverage I love:

Daryl Groom, whose hysterical tales often left me doubled over laughing.

Gary Eberle, whose blue dress, along with his commitment to the community and the industry, is legendary.

David Stevens, whose technical expertise has been invaluable.

Lois Henry and Aimee Barajas, "agents" extraordinaire.

Klaus Hoeper, with whom I've traveled many a mile and enjoyed many a glass.

The late Justin Meyer, who always shared his expertise and sense of humor.

Toby Shumrick, a good sport and funny guy.

Chuck Ortman, with whom I occasionally got lost in the wrong parts of towns and lived to laugh about it.

Dan Berger, who has more funny stories than most people know.

Mike Rubin, who with his wife, Linda, provided inspiration and encouragement.

Bob Thompson, whose wisdom and knowledge inspired me to learn.

Jill Ditmire, whose joy for life is infectious.

Dick Vine, aka Dr. Richard Vine, who had faith in me and encouraged me.

Joe Hart, with whom I've judged many a wine and enjoyed many a glass.

Dick Peterson, aka Dr. Richard Peterson, who never stops giving of himself.

Craig Goldwyn, who helped launch my wine experience.

Wilfred Wong, whose olfactory talents match his "Giant" joviality.

Bob Foster, a gentleman, scholar, and superb palate.

Larry Gomez, whose laughter and generosity know no bounds.

Don Galleano, whose love for and commitment to the industry inspires.

Mitch Cosentino, whose golf game is almost as good as his wines.

Pierre Freeman, "oenotarian" extraordinaire.

The late Carol Stepanovich, whose sense of adventure infected this tale.

A special thank-you to my editor, Lois Henry, whose editing talents and insights in writing this story were invaluable. It's better because of her. I can't thank her enough.

And an extra special thank-you to Patt Davis, whose patience, kindness, guidance and support brought this book to reality.

ZINFORADO!

About the Author

Wine journalist Mike Stepanovich has been covering the wine industry since 1985 and judging wines since 1987. Mike is an avid wine collector who also teaches wine history, wine appreciation and wine-and-food-pairing classes.

His work has appeared in such national and international publications as *International Wine Review*, *Wine News* and *Wine Business Monthly*.

He travels extensively and has reported on wine developments in Europe as well as the United States.

Mike has judged numerous wine competitions including the American Wine Competition, Indianapolis International Wine Competition, Florida International Wine Competition, Pacific Rim International Wine Competition, Riverside International Wine Competition, San Francisco International Wine Competition, San Diego International Wine Competition and Long Beach Grand Cru.

He made wine from grapes he grew himself and from other sources from 2000 to 2012.

He resides in Bakersfield, California.

CPSIA information can be obtained
at www.ICGtesting.com
Printed in the USA
LVHW082344190722
723926LV00028B/894